SECRET HISTORIES

THE DSA SEASON TWO, BOOK FIVE

SECRET HISTORIES

Lou Paduano

Eleven Ten Publishing LLC

GRAND ISLAND, NEW YORK

Eleven Ten Publishing LLC
282 Fareway Lane
Grand Island, NY 14072

Publisher's note: This is a work of fiction. Names, characters, places, and incidents either are the product of the author's imagination or are used fictitiously. Any resemblance to actual events, locales, or persons, living or dead, is entirely coincidental.

Printed in the United States of America
Edited by JP Services.
Cover art design by MiblArt

First edition published 2024

Library of Congress Cataloguing in Publication Data
Paduano, Lou
Secret Histories / Lou Paduano

LCCN: 2024912890
ISBN-13: 978-1-944965-45-7 (paperback)
ISBN-13: 978-1-944965-44-0 (eBook)

For Aaron

CHAPTER ONE

Never surrender. Robert Kanigher's father taught him that at a young age. The mantra had served the boy well over the years, at the playground or in sports. He had carried it with him through multiple tours overseas, using his wits to keep those close to him safe from harm.

Surrender now seemed inevitable, however. The thought stabbed through him worse than a knife to the heart. Sweat dotted Kanigher's brow. His hands were slick to the touch, and no amount of rubbing along his pants stopped the flow. His breath caught in his throat, tense along his shoulders and back.

"This is stupid," he muttered. The elevator whirred upward. Lights beamed from the sides of the underground car as the elevator rose to the surface from the Bunker. The words needed to be said. More were necessary, but they fell flat when he ran them through his mind.

The figure before him didn't bother to turn around. She continued to stare straight ahead; blonde hair hid her reaction. With a bowed head, she waited for the ding of the elevator car and the opening of the doors. Her fate waited outside, and there wasn't a damn thing Kanigher could do to help her.

"This was your idea," Susan Metcalf said.

Kanigher tried to laugh, but sorrow drowned the jest. "Why do you think I said it?"

The car stopped with a jolt. On instinct, Kanigher reached for the closest wall, then stopped. The woman in front of him made no motion at all.

Doors opened. Daylight shifted inside, blanketing the car with the early afternoon sun. Warm air greeted them, leaving all thought of the winter buried in the past. It would have made for a terrific day. Kanigher felt the calm wind along his cheeks and wondered if things would ever feel so good again. The day should have been theirs to seize, to embrace a quiet moment and savor every second.

But that was not to be, nor would such a serene day have been possible. Too much had occurred of late between the team. There had been too many secrets, all on Metcalf's side, and all culminated in the truth about her relationship with a man known to them as the Witness.

Because of Metcalf, and her innate ability to hide the truth from those around her, everything the DSA had worked for over the years had shattered. Kanigher wanted nothing more than to believe they could work through her secrets to find a road back to the way things had been. It would take time, however, and time had run out for them.

"It's too open out there," Kanigher said. His hand shot out for the figure at the door. It fell away with his gaze, unable to bear looking at her. "We'll be sitting ducks."

"Not you," Metcalf said. "Me."

She made no move. Her shadow fell upon him as the sunlight washed over her. She didn't turn to look at him with those cold-as-steel-blue eyes that somehow always burrowed straight to his soul. He just wanted to see them one last time.

"Susan, I'm sorry about—"

"Let's get this over with, Bobby," Metcalf interrupted. The words had already been spoken, the arguments nothing but circular motions of redundancy. Everything had passed between them over the years. Nothing remained to change what was coming.

The woman left the elevator behind. Daylight enveloped her slender frame. Kanigher crept toward the door. He made no motion to leave, the instructions clear before their arrival. This was for her, and her alone.

"Good luck," he called after her, knowing the futility of his words.

Neither had ever truly believed in luck. For her, skill and tactics were all that mattered. For Kanigher, it was his father's dictum repeating in his brain.

Never surrender.

He knew better now. That had been the ideal of a child, not the compromising nature of an adult. And while Kanigher hated believing his father to be nothing more than a fool, the proof stood before him in the field that ran between the Bunker and the farmhouse outside.

Metcalf made it less than ten steps into the open before a shot cracked the silence of the peaceful afternoon. The gunshot slammed into the woman's chest. Her body swayed from the impact, and for a moment Kanigher believed her to be okay—that somehow the bullet missed and her reaction had been nothing but instinctual.

Then she fell. No noise left her; no cry of pain or shriek of terror slipped from her lips. Susan Metcalf merely fell to the soft, green earth and didn't move again.

CHAPTER TWO
Six Hours Earlier

Metcalf scanned the room. For as much as all eyes were on her, her own took in each player. They believed they understood the reason for her presence, but she knew with absolute certainty why each of them had made their way into the Bunker—and onto her team.

She knew them too well.

Metcalf had recruited them at their lowest. The failures were not their own, yet they carried them like scars from a forsaken battle. In Morgan Dunleavy's case, it had come from conflict—the near-death of her brother, and the sacrifice of three lives to save him. Her brother had spurned her gift of life, and when he'd turned his back on her, she'd lost her own.

Morgan's anger at Metcalf came from her role as a medic. It started from knowing Metcalf's actions over the years had led to the deaths of dozens, if not hundreds. Learning about Metcalf's connection to the Witness had been the last straw. His experiment in Bellbrook had cost thousands their lives and wiped a town from existence.

That last lie put Kanigher against Metcalf as well. Bobby had always been by her side, working through the NSA to further her department's agenda. Kanigher had been unwavering in his loyalty for as long as she had known him. There had been genuine friendship between them, tied together thanks to Jacob Grissom at the start before they truly connected on their own.

Ever since finding out about the Witness, Kanigher struggled to look directly at Metcalf for more than a second at a stretch. When he did, his eyes were full of sadness and disappointment at being kept in the dark. Her secrets had betrayed a friendship that dated back almost a decade.

How could she think it would do any less to those she had only known for months, if not weeks? Nixon Jessup fell into the latter. She'd recruited him under false pretenses by creating the circumstances for his arrest by local law enforcement. At the same time, she had promised to rescue him in exchange for his skills. He was now a mere bystander in the argument, yet even his opinion weighed on her mind.

Alison Adler stayed quiet in the corner. She certainly carried her own opinion. Metcalf had brought her in because of her innate ability to read a situation. While Metcalf scanned the room to see where her team fell in their judgment of her actions, Adler did the same. It separated her from the others, always knowing which way the wind was going to blow before the breeze accidentally sent you sailing off the cliff. It was why she'd done as well as she had as an undercover operative before Metcalf had brought her in for tactical.

All of them carried their own opinions. They all sought to blame or forgive Metcalf for the secrets she kept. None had become more confused over the course of their relationship than Ben Riley. He'd hated her secrets—known about them sooner than anyone else in the room—yet he had offered her a way out. He'd begged her to tell the rest and given her time to do so.

She'd failed, and in doing so, failed Ben. Still, his eyes wavered on her. It came from an undue loyalty to his father, another of Metcalf's secrets, but also the second chance she had offered him with the DSA.

To Metcalf, each held her fate in their hands—and with it, the fate of the DSA. For as much as they sought an intervention over her secrets, this was much more.

This was a tribunal.

"We need the truth," Ben said. He broke the silence, the one thing he disliked more than the secrets. He sat at the head of the conference table in the Bunker. His words drew no looks. All eyes stayed with Metcalf, who remained at the top of the short flight of stairs above the Operations Hub in their underground headquarters. "We're long past the secrets and the lies of Susan Metcalf."

"You get that, don't you, Susan?" Kanigher asked. Pain filled his deep voice. "You understand why we are where we are now? Why we have no choice but to figure out a way forward?"

"With or without you," Morgan finished. The woman's own judgment had clearly already been made. Morgan held too much rage for Metcalf, from the death of Grissom all the way to the loss of Lincoln MacKenzie.

"I do." Metcalf offered a nod of acceptance at their assertions. "I understand."

"You knew the Witness," Ben said. It was the reason for their meeting. The time for lies had long since passed, and it was time for the truth. At least the truth, as far as she was willing to give it.

"I did, yes."

"How long?" Kanigher asked.

Morgan shook her head. The question didn't go far enough for her. "Was it before Bellbrook?"

Metcalf stared into the thin eyes of her subordinate. "Yes."

Murmurs picked up from Nixon and Adler. Shared glances passed between the five surrounding the table—her judge, jury, and executioners, if they deemed necessary.

Ben slowly stood, hands tight against the edge of the table. "Yet you said nothing."

"I attempted to rectify my error," Metcalf said, hands clasped against her back. "I failed."

"And Lincoln died," Morgan snapped. She jumped to her feet and moved to the stairs. Her hand slammed down on the railing. "Would he have died if you were straight with him? With any of us?"

"Morgan," Ben called. Her rising anger stymied his attempt to draw her back to the table. "That's not fair. She didn't know what was going to happen to Lincoln. That was Sullivan."

"Don't defend her, Ben," Morgan said through clenched teeth. Her eyes stayed with Metcalf. "You have just as much to be upset about. The Witness killed Ruth Heller. He almost killed you!"

"He also saved me," Ben shot back as he circled the table for the opposite railing. "I don't quite understand why, but there's more going on here. Isn't there, Metcalf?"

There always had been. Metcalf knew it better than most and had since the very beginning of her journey.

*****

Most people were born into the world. They came as infants and proceeded through the natural order of events from birth to death. Metcalf wasn't born in such terms, but forged by the choices she made. If asked, she would have said her first actual memory was nothing as cheerful as a Sunday picnic with her family, or the opening pitch of a baseball game.

Metcalf's first memory was of leaving her life behind.

"You can't just walk away from this, Suzie!" her brother Brendan shouted after her. The screen door slammed behind her. The backpack clutched tight to her shoulder, heavy with the clothes she'd packed hurriedly. "I need your help to run this place, and you said—"

"I never said!" Metcalf yelled. Her paltry sixteen-year-old voice cracked in tune with the thunder in the distance. "You said. Just like always."

"Suzie…"

"No," she spat. "I can't stay. I won't be stuck here. Like you. I won't!"

More had been said leading up to her departure. Too many words passed between them, filled with anger and hate, but none carried the weight and the finality as those last ones spoken to a brother only trying to hold their lives together in the wake of their parents' deaths. Nothing held her there, though, and nothing ever would.

Following her swift escape from the farmhouse, Metcalf traveled north. She worked for scraps and bummed rides from strangers to get as far away from Odenton—and responsibility—as possible. Along the way, she lived in dingy rooms with dozens of others. Metcalf barely slept for fear of losing what little she'd brought with her, only to have it happen when exhaustion finally won out.

Even through her mistakes, Metcalf continued to try to find a place for herself. Her travels took her all the way to Western New York. Along a deserted street, in the dead of night, Metcalf questioned her last words to her brother. All thought, however, fell silent when a hand reached out of the darkness and grabbed her.

Metcalf never saw the face of her attacker, merely his shadow. When she woke from that assault, she found herself caged. It was small, forcing her to sit or lie curled up in a ball. Her legs ached from the lack of movement. Her body screamed from the discomfort at finding itself naked.

She suffered in the cage for weeks. Hands tormented her body. A hose washed her cell clean every day, but could not wipe away the stain of the acts committed against her.

There were others too. She noted five other voices in the darkness. They cried through the night, or prayed for death to end their suffering. Metcalf remained quiet, her world nothing more than a blur as her mind retreated from the daily abuse inflicted upon her by her captor.

Over time, she noticed the girls in the dark. They were young like her, hardly women in some respects. Fear filled their eyes from a loss of control. Metcalf refused to be afraid, to be weak in the face of her abductor, no matter the lack of food or sleep.

One night, things changed. Instead of the usual taunts from the shadows before the abuse came for all others to witness, each girl was taken from their cage in turn. A bright light shone on each victim, right before they were ripped from the darkness in a swift motion. Metcalf prepared for the end to come her way. The second the light shifted her way, and the cage door opened, Metcalf kicked out at her captor. Fingers grasped tight to the sides of her cage. Metal ripped at her flesh, smearing blood across her hands.

"No!" she cried. "I won't let you!"

No leery eyes washed over her. Only a hand reached out from the light. "I'm not going to hurt you," the man said. "I'm here to help."

She didn't believe it, not after the endless desecration. Metcalf shifted deeper into her cage, desperate to remain out of the light. Her fear threatened to win out. Then she saw the truth in the man's eyes—soft and restrained—and in the glinting metal of the badge pinned to his chest.

"Take my hand, kiddo," he said. "I've got you."

Metcalf reached toward the light. Her body felt weightless as the man lifted her from the cage. She held him tight, spreading blood along his silk tie. He wrapped her up in a blanket, then carried her from the ramshackle hut that had been her prison. The other girls were outside, all huddled together for support. In the back of the police cruiser sat her captor, his face still nothing but shadows, but in the darkness his crazed stare fell on her.

She never learned his name, afraid to give a face to a nightmare that would haunt her forever. Instead, she focused on the man who had saved her life—who had, in fact, granted her a second chance at a life yet to be lived.

His name was Kenneth Riley.

"You're safe now."

It was the absolute truth, and she refused to waste another moment of her life. She never wanted to experience that loss of control again—to be powerless and broken. This was her second chance, and she was going to make the most of it.

Her mistakes now threatened to wipe away all the good she'd hoped to accomplish with her second chance. Her time in the cage made it impossible to trust in those around her. The walls built up from that experience had led her to hide away all the important things… and to this tribunal.

"You can judge my actions as you will," Metcalf said, still standing tall and proud over her colleagues. "I stand by every one. They led me to you—to this. To the DSA. Despite my failings, despite my errors. Don't forget that."

She didn't need to hear another word. She didn't need to feel the eyes of judgment from those around her. Their rage and their pity followed her from the stairs toward the dormitory.

"Where are you going?" Morgan asked, the anger still prominent in her voice.

Metcalf turned back. "Have your discussion. Decide my fate. But I won't stand here and defend myself like a criminal."

"Susan," Kanigher called.

Her head fell low. A hand shot out to the nearby wall for support. "Make your choice, Bobby."

CHAPTER THREE

She had disabled the locks weeks ago. Finding the place had been the laborious task, but once she'd learned the name of the woman behind all her troubles, things quickly lined up. Property deeds, public notes of sale, and other properly filed documents had been located, and the trail suddenly made complete sense.

Patience had brought Vivian Ness to her moment of revenge. How she'd ever found such a well of infinite patience was beyond her, yet now her time had come.

The farmhouse held little value for her on the surface. Days had been spent combing through each room. She had pulled at every decoration on the walls and dug through the dust-ridden floors for some sign of life. Something more hid here, something other than the so-called American dream of white-picket fences around a yellow-sided domicile.

A switch tucked behind the banister to the second floor revealed the truth. The wall shifted, kicking away the dust and decay of neglect, and gave way to a computer control room far beyond any Vivian had seen before. Monitors adorned the walls. It appeared the entire compound was rife with surveillance. A security measure, perhaps, but it allowed her a window into the soul of her target.

Securing the room behind her, Vivian settled in for the actual work. Time slipped away from her, but with it came an intimate knowledge of the system. She knew how to take control, how to dismantle the security of the underground structure hidden in the back of the property.

Her study of the control room also brought her a new understanding of every player on the screens. From the young woman with the glasses and her stringent work ethic to the late-night snacking of a shabbily dressed man with a penchant for reading comic books, Vivian viewed the entire Bunker and the personnel working within.

None of the others mattered, though. They were bit players in the drama that encapsulated Vivian's life. Her hand slipped from the keyboard and moved for her right eye. Fingers vanished from her view, her sight long since destroyed by the acts of the woman at the heart of her rage. Revenge was all that was left to Vivian Ness, and she would have it on the woman who stole away her life.

Darkness consumed her world. Stirring to consciousness, she found herself lost in a haze. She blinked rapidly to shake away the cobwebs that seemed to settle over her entire being. A dim light showered over her from a nearby lamp on her left. Beeping rose from her right; machines clicked and whirred, but when she glanced over, she saw nothing but darkness.

Panic set in. She couldn't see. Her vision failed on the right. Turning her head slightly, she realized it was only on the right as her left picked up the monitors in the hospital room.

What happened? Why am I here?

A dozen more questions raced through her mind. She tried to move, to escape whatever was being done to her, only to find her body unwilling. Her limbs held no strength, the time spent in the hospital bed extensive.

At her movements, sudden voices grew in the corridor. Steps quickened in her direction as two women approached with stunned looks on their faces.

"Ella esta volviendo," one said. "Llama al doctor."

She's coming around. Get the doctor.

The words made complete sense to her somehow. She recognized them to be Spanish, yet instinctively realized they did not match her own native tongue. She reached for her head. The grogginess was too strong to shake.

The other nurse slipped from the room. She closed the curtain on her way out, leaving the pair with their privacy. The young woman at her bedside set to work.

"What... happened?"

The question came from a voice that surprised even the bed-ridden patient from which it originated. Her words were weak and despondent, pitiful attempts to gain traction in the world to which she had woken up to. Continuing with her task, the nurse leaned closer.

"English," she said with a slight nod. "I do my best."

"Where?" the patient asked, the word stronger this time. The voice, however, remained strange to her own ear. "Where am I?"

"Hospital. You hurt very bad."

The curtain pulled back. A doctor strode in, dark-skinned, with gray along the temples and in his thick beard. He started toward the right side of the bed, then stopped. Rounding the other side, he cut in front of the nurse.

"I have this," he said. The woman completed her note, then passed along the small chart. "Thank you."

Sympathetic eyes met the patient, pity at her situation. She hated the look and was glad when the nurse closed the curtain behind her once more.

"How are you feeling?" His English was better, clearly having studied in his youth and maintained the skill during his time at the medical center.

"Terrible," the woman replied. "My head is pounding, and I can't—" Her hand settled over her right eye. A bandage covered it. "Is this why I can't see? I need to—"

"Don't," the doctor said. He forced her hand away from the bandage. He brought it down to rest at her side. "You suffered a terrible injury."

"I… I don't remember."

The past was a blank spot in her memory. There was nothing but white space when she went to access the incident that had brought her to the hospital. Loud and terrible sounds, like the ringing of bells, filled her senses. She cringed at the sound, her headache worse for the attempt.

"I can't remember," she said again.

The doctor looked her over with a sad nod. "Yes. That is not uncommon for someone with your trauma."

"Tell me."

He pointed to the bandage on her eye. "The bullet took your right eye, but the angle of the shot did minimal damage beneath the surface. You've been in a coma since they found you."

"A coma?" Another question came up behind the first, one she kept to herself. What the hell had she been doing to earn a bullet to the head? The woman struggled to sit up taller. "How long?"

"Six months."

"Six…" She shook her head. Her legs screamed as she tried to inch toward the edge of the bed. "I have to—"

"Rest." The doctor stopped her once more. She slowly settled back against her pillows. "You have to rest."

"I…" She surrendered to the notion. Her body sided with the doctor, easing back into the depressed cushion where she had lain for months.

"Is there anyone we can contact?" the doctor asked. "You had no ID, no phone on you when they found you."

"Anyone?" Her mind begged for a response. She tried to pull the name of a loved one—family or friend—anyone who might be worried about her. "I don't remember."

"Perhaps if you gave us your name, we could—"

"My name?" Fear filled her. Panic consumed her. A white void was all that remained in her mind. "I can't remember my name. I can't remember anything."

It took years for Vivian to come back from that day. They were years of patience, built from anger and bitterness.

All had been for today. All the suffering and struggle was for her revenge on the woman who stole her life from her. Before the day was through, Susan Metcalf would meet her end.

Only then could Vivian Ness live again.

CHAPTER FOUR

"Move."

The hand was on Zac Modine's arm before he could follow the direction. It shoved Zac from the back seat of the passenger van. When he fell toward the concrete, another hand jutted out to stop his descent. The act was a small comfort as the pair of government stooges prodded their captive into a standing position before knocking him toward yet another warehouse.

Ever since his capture, Zac had seen several just like it. Grand Island, Nebraska might have been in the rearview, but it didn't stop the scenic tour of clandestine facilities on their journey.

Zac understood the need behind the constant movement. It followed the same pattern as the lack of food, and even less sleep, over the last couple of days. All were meant to disorient him and keep him off balance.

Few words had been spoken during his travels. At least, few had come from the guards except for the strictest of instructions to be followed to the letter. Outward communication might have been lackluster, but the voice in Zac's head still kept him company. April Newton continued to make her presence known; she made it clear the process had yet to finish.

The Wellspring Protocol slowly consumed Zac. He could do nothing to stop it, not while in the grasp of the Trust. The only way out of his current predicament was escape, something the number of guns constantly aimed in his direction made impossible. Yet, that was the only way for Zac to locate the signal that may serve as his salvation.

Bismarck. I have to get to Bismarck and find it.

The two guards spurred Zac to the elevator in the back of the warehouse. Where loading bays dominated the lowest level of the building, they soon gave way to carpet and pristine, painted walls. Clearly in an office building, Zac shuffled his way into the elevator. One of the men slammed a finger on the button to ascend, and the car shook in compliance.

Their journey took them to the thirty-second floor of the building. Light showered through the doors when they opened. Large windows marked the end of the hallways. Zac caught sight of a building or two in the distance, but nothing as tall as their current whereabouts. Reading his hesitation, another hand fell against his back to prod Zac forward.

An office across the corridor opened for him. Waiting inside with hands in his pockets and a smile on his face was David Hollis, the head of the Trust.

"Glad you could make it, Zac," Hollis announced upon his arrival. He rounded his desk, set before a row of windows overlooking the city below, with outstretched hands. "So glad to have you here."

"Like I had a choice."

Hollis ignored the comment. He wrapped an arm around Zac. A stiff glare to the guards told them enough to vacate the room, leaving only the pair to chat. Hollis guided Zac over to the windows.

"How are you feeling this morning?" he asked. "Did you have a pleasant drive in?"

Zac hesitated. He grew tired of the game, especially the constant need to keep him off balance. The smug look on Hollis' face reminded Zac that the game was all they had left, so he played along.

"It was fine."

Hollis nodded, clearly reading Zac's reluctance to speak up. "Good to hear."

Zac kept his eyes on the window. For as much as his vision had been blocked, and the travel constant over the last two days, all it took was one glance and he knew his exact location. The information came from the Wellspring locked in his brain, a gift that came with a delightful headache and the threat of permanently overriding his own identity.

Zac recognized the skyline of Lincoln, Nebraska, as if he had lived there his entire life. From his vantage point, Zac made out three notable landmarks immediately. The Nebraska State Capitol building soared in the distance, away from all other structures. Outdoor sculptures occupied the grounds surrounding the Sheldon Museum of Art. To the west of the museum was Pinnacle Bank Arena, the home of the Huskers.

More than understanding his surroundings, Zac realized the building itself to be Trust Compound Number 243. While the former might have been drawn by some innate knowledge of the area, the building itself was intel unlocked by the Wellspring. He glanced around the room and noted every access point. In a blink, the entire layout of the building was laid out before him, as well as the surrounding neighbors down to the tenant in each location and their lease details.

"Magnificent views." Hollis slapped at Zac's shoulder. "I love coming here."

He turned away from the window, a nod for the door. "I have us set up in the next room. Want a cup of coffee?"

Zac continued to stare outside. Information flooded his senses. The sudden influx of knowledge made him want to scream, yet he held the pain in check. The process was getting easier, a thought that rattled Zac to his core.

"No dawdling, Zac," Hollis said. "I don't want to have to shoot you."

The threat was enough to end Zac's rumination. He had seen enough death at the hands of Hollis and his men. Visions of Henry Reed's lifeless body played before his eyes. Zac's gaze thinned when he met Hollis near the door. "Yeah. I wouldn't want that."

The connecting door opened. Inside was a windowless office. A desk sat near the wall with paper and pen tucked in the corner. Two chairs, one on each side, were positioned for them. Hollis extended his hand, offering one to Zac. The captive made his way over and settled against the hard metal base. The guards returned. One carried a steaming beverage and let it rest before Zac.

"See? Coffee," Hollis said. A silent nod to the guards left them the room once more. Hollis sat across from Zac, his left leg crossing over his right—completely at ease and in control.

Zac stared at the coffee. The lack of meals since his capture had certainly left him feeling peckish and parched. Nonetheless, he refused to reach for the cup.

"It's not poison or anything, Zac." A befuddled expression arose on the man's face. Hollis held up a finger. Standing, he moved for the door. Hollis ducked his head outside. "It's not poison, is it?"

"Sir?"

Hollis laughed. "Nothing. A joke with my friend here." Hollis closed the door and returned to his seat. "It's hard to keep track of the details sometimes."

"I'm sure."

Hollis shook his head, eyes steady on Zac. "I'm loving this new you, Zac. The dry wit. The stoic resistance. It's an honest reaction, and I hope I can respond in kind. Would that be all right?"

"Do I have a choice?"

"No," Hollis answered. It caused a smile to spread across his face. "See? Honest. And I can honestly say, Zac, old boy, that you look like crap. Fall did that to you?"

Zac barely felt the pain anymore. The one in his head was that much worse. Zac's capture had come in the aftermath of his leap off a four-story building. His foolish move had been to evade his pursuers, including the late Henry Reed. The adjacent building had been the goal, albeit one just out of reach.

The fall left Zac with several bruised ribs, numerous scrapes that ran up and down his arms and legs, and an enormous purple welt hidden under his shirt. He'd only survived thanks to the massive pile of refuse in the alley.

"How bad does it hurt?" Hollis asked, false concern wrapped in his sadistic grin.

"Some."

A nod of understanding left Hollis before the man leaned in closer to the desk. He took the coffee in hand and sipped at the still-steaming beverage. "Not enough sleep? Too much stress? Why don't we fix that for you, huh? It's a simple enough solution. The Wellspring. I want her. You know where she is."

This time, it was Zac who laughed. It startled Hollis. At the sound, Zac stopped himself, then rubbed at his weary eyes. Hollis wanted the Wellspring—still believed her to be alive, in fact—but she had lost her life at the Cove over a month earlier. Hollis didn't know, couldn't know, what had happened or what came after thanks to Zac's proximity to the deceased.

The head of the Trust lowered his coffee. It slammed against the desk, contents spilling over the lip. Cold eyes met Zac's. "She serves a role, Zac. Funny or not, without the Wellspring to guide the way, we are all diminished for it."

"Guide our way to what?" The question kept Zac up at night and had ever since he'd learned about the Wellspring.

Hollis leaned back in his chair. "A golden age of prosperity. Paradise on Earth."

"Through order and control," Zac shot back. "Your control."

"Order keeps us going, Zac," Hollis said. "Always has, always will. If I'm not steering the ship, someone else is. The destination never changes."

Zac waited. He read the arrogance in Hollis' face. This man truly believed he was the only one able to handle the responsibility of safeguarding the future. Looking into the man's blistering brown eyes, Zac realized something else as well.

"You don't know either, do you?" he said with a smile. "She never told you what's coming."

Hollis' jaw clenched. "Where is she?"

"No idea," Zac replied. His arms crossed his chest, and he settled back against the uncomfortable chair. "I sure as hell wouldn't share it with you."

Hollis slapped the coffee aside. The cup slammed against the wall, then crashed to the floor. A line of liquid ran to join the cup along the carpet. Hollis rounded the desk quickly. Raising his hand, Hollis wound up, then smacked Zac across the face.

The blow drove Zac off the chair and to the ground. Pain shot across Zac's cheek from the impact. His hand shifted to touch the wound, and he noticed he was bleeding. Zac turned to face his attacker to see Hollis fixing the ring along his finger. A needle along one side glittered with a dab of red under the lights of the office.

Hollis allowed a deep breath, before clasping his hands behind his back. "Now, I've always considered myself something of a civilized man. Violence of any sort is never necessary. All I want is answers, Zac. It can be that simple. A conversation between old friends. Or, it can get very complicated."

Zac swiped at his cheek. "I won't help you. Just kill me and get it over with."

"You should know better than that, Zac. Killing you means nothing. Thankfully, I have other means to convince you to talk."

Hollis laughed as he moved for the door. He exited the room quickly without another word.

Zac struggled to sit upright. Every inch of his body was in agony. Still, his pain was nothing compared to what he felt when the door opened once more. Hollis returned, dragging someone behind him by the wrist.

"Zac?" the woman's voice called.

Zac's eyes widened. He hadn't seen her in weeks. Every memory came flooding back to him the second her voice reached him.

"Claire?" he said. It was his wife. Hollis grabbed her by the arm and held her close. His fingers locked around her neck. "Let her go, you son of a—"

Hollis squeezed tighter. "No threats, Zac. Not now."

"What—"

Hollis shoved Zac's wife deeper into the office. "I'll leave you to weigh your options, Zac. As limited as they are."

He slammed the door on them. The lock clicked loudly from outside. There was no way out. With his wife now involved, his impossible escape became even more dangerous. Zac's options weren't merely limited, they didn't exist at all.

CHAPTER FIVE

Metcalf paced her private quarters impatiently. Every thought, every wish and dream and nightmare combined, centered on the discussion around the conference table. For a time, she had tried to listen in. Her irritation at their argument, however, had made that impossible. The back and forth between her hand-selected team had forced her to close herself off in her room rather than be swept up in their fury over her decisions.

A sigh escaped her, and she stopped at the back of her room. A hand fell against the side of her bed's headboard, putting all her weight on the object to relieve the heaviness she felt throughout her body.

She didn't blame her team. All fault rested with her. She'd allowed the division to take root. Her inability to trust damned them all a second time after watching the first burn to the ground thanks to Sullivan's infiltration.

Their judgment was unnecessary. Her own was clear, an anchor tied to her ankle—to their collective ankle. The DSA needed to be better, and she didn't know if such a thing was possible for her. After all the years of secrets, Metcalf found it difficult to find a way back.

She started to push the bed aside when a knock at the door interrupted her. Metcalf turned at the sound, startled when the knob turned.

Kanigher stepped inside. He carried a tray with a carefully prepared meal of leafy greens and steamed vegetables: one of her favorites.

"I made lunch," he said with a sad smile. "May I?"

Metcalf shifted away from the wall, her steps staggered. She glanced back toward the bed, then continued with a nod to her guest. "Of course."

"What were you doing?" Kanigher pointed toward the shifted headboard.

"Nothing," she replied without looking. Metcalf moved for the door and closed it behind Kanigher. "So, what's the verdict?"

She kept the tone light, though her words clearly stung the man. No one wanted to have the conversation. Circumstance had thrust it upon them. To continue without action merely courted the same disaster that ended the last incarnation of the DSA. Metcalf knew the danger of her secrets, and paid for them with each stolen glance and each deep breath from the man who stood as her closest friend in the world.

Kanigher set the tray down. He looked around the room. The place was spartan, just the way she liked it. Her needs were minimal, matched by the time spent in her room. It was the way she had been since her belongings were stolen as a teen.

"Bobby?" The question drew him back from his snooping.

Kanigher sighed. "No idea. They took a break. Adler needed to get back to her hunt for that mystery signal. She might be obsessed, or it's just a nice distraction from things. Nixon decided to help. He thinks if they can restart the mainframe, the system will be able to lock onto the signal easier."

"Sounds dangerous."

Kanigher shrugged. "According to the genius, not so much. There might be a few outages here or there, but nothing catastrophic."

"Which you don't believe for a second," Metcalf chided. She took a seat at the desk. An open hand offered the bed to her company.

"When Nixon says a few, I expect complete and total."

Metcalf picked at the steamed vegetables on the tray. She popped a carrot into her mouth and smiled. "And the others?"

"Arguing," Kanigher said as he sat at the end of the bed. "That seems to be their standard, as far as I can tell."

"So you cooked."

"It helps me think," Kanigher said. "It's not much, but—"

"It's perfect. Thank you."

She dug into the salad. Thick romaine, mixed with cucumbers, carrots, radishes, and chickpeas, settled between her lips. A moan of satisfaction escaped, and she quickly reached for the napkin tucked beneath the plate to wipe her face of the excess ranch dressing.

"You always told me you cooked to help you 'score with the ladies,'" Metcalf said with a laugh.

Kanigher shook his head, a hand to his brow. "God. Did I really say that?"

"A lifetime ago."

They were words shared during the early days, when plans had been made for a better tomorrow. They were days of dreams, full of light and hope. Naïve dreams, perhaps, but both of them bonded from their sharing. Metcalf couldn't help but wonder how the dreams slipped away, and if she was as much to blame for that as she was for their current predicament.

"What did your thinking conclude?" she asked. His gaze fell away, his hands clenched tight to his knees. "I don't want to know, do I?"

Kanigher let out a deep breath, then stood. "I came to help, Susan, because I believe in the mission. I used to believe in you. Your secrets—"

She raised a hand to stop him. Metcalf understood, and didn't need to hear the words from him. She knew them by heart.

"They have a price, Bobby," she said. "They always have a price."

CHAPTER SIX
Sixteen Years Ago

The kick sailed wide. Metcalf felt the wind rush by her from the blow, then shifted away from her opponent. Tucking into a roll, she moved for open space.

Aggravation filled her opponent, a fellow recruit with over seventy pounds on her as well as a six-inch height advantage. Michael Daye's dislike of Metcalf was well known, and when the sparring exercise hit the schedule at Quantico, Michael was more than happy to sign up to take her down a peg.

Four minutes into the bout, however, he had yet to land a strike against her. She read his physicality as a weakness rather than a strength. Arrogant to a fault, Michael brought baggage into the ring. Metcalf, though, brought only her wits.

It was what had led her to Quantico. After everything that had happened to her in New York, and with the guidance of Kenneth Riley, Metcalf had quickly realized law enforcement was the perfect career path for her. It offered a chance to take back control of her life and seize her own inner strength.

That strategy kept her on her feet during the fight. Michael rushed for her again, his left arm cocked back for an attack. Metcalf read the blow coming her way. She ducked under it, then drove up with her fist. It slammed into Michael's chin. The suddenness and timing of the strike caused the young man to stagger back.

Michael stayed on his feet, though his eyes glazed over. He shook off the effects, his frustration winning out over all common sense. When he looked at Metcalf, all he saw was a woman—weak and unprepared for the work of the FBI or any law enforcement agency.

He failed to realize the education Metcalf had endured since her abduction at the age of sixteen. Years of martial arts training, multiple self-defense classes, as well as months spent learning at various gun ranges, had opened up Metcalf's eyes to her own potential. She knew her body better than anyone and never stepped into the ring unprepared.

Michael lashed out with another driving blow. His strength came at a cost, but he never saw it. The moment the fist swayed in front of a backpedaling Metcalf, she grabbed his arm. Using his momentum, Metcalf lifted Michael over her shoulder and slammed him to the ground. Working to tie up his extremities, Metcalf pinned Michael's arm behind his back, and locked his legs under her own. A sharp cry of pain escaped her opponent before the whistle blew behind them.

Metcalf dropped the man's arm and stood. She held out her hand, which was promptly swatted away by Michael. The coordinator for the group called two more opponents to the ring as Metcalf made her way to the sideline to watch.

"Cadet!" a uniformed officer yelled from the door. "Metcalf!"

"Sir?" Metcalf asked, curious. She still had an hour of training before another afternoon of classes.

"Upstairs wants to see you." The woman passed along a note. Metcalf read the name listed, surprise in her eyes.

"Any idea why?"

"Not a one." She smiled as she escorted Metcalf to the door. "Nice takedown, by the way. He might think twice next time."

"That's the thing," Metcalf said, shooting Michael a smug grin. "He won't."

Metcalf made the trip to the fourth floor of the building. It was reserved for ambassadors and advisors alike, offices of the highest order to visiting professionals. Upon arrival, Metcalf offered the man a stiff salute.

Seated behind the desk was a tall, slender man in a pale suit. He wore thin reading glasses. Light shone off his bald head. His frame might have been perceived as a weakness, or that of a bureaucrat more than a soldier, but Metcalf knew better than to make the assumption. Anson Greene was anything but weak. As a special advisor, the man held more power than most four-star generals.

Metcalf stood upright. "You wanted to see me, sir?"

A nod calmed her posture. "Have a seat," the man said in a calm, detached voice.

She did so, and silence returned to the room. Behind her, the door closed to allow them their privacy. Greene went about his work as if she was not present. He flipped through files on his desk and made notes when necessary.

The man was a ghost to most. No one knew exactly what his role entailed at Quantico, or anywhere really. Greene had a hand in every cookie jar the government put a name to, every agency from coast to coast, but no one understood why he was needed or what he added to the team. Rumors persisted he was the true power behind the government—like the great Oz behind the curtain who controlled the destiny of the country.

Metcalf's presence in the same room with him concerned her, yet also filled her with a dangerous excitement. He muttered under his breath, and she leaned closer to the desk. "Did you say something, sir?"

Greene lowered his readers to the desk. "Six months in?"

"Yes, sir."

"Enjoying it?"

Metcalf hesitated. The man's eyes held her full attention, probing for information. She cleared her throat and straightened her back against the chair. "As much as I can."

Greene nodded. His understanding was immediate. "Your testing shows extreme aptitude. You're highly intuitive. You've shown innovative tactics and problem solving. I can only imagine how bored you are here."

"I don't—"

"It's all right, Metcalf," Greene said with a calm wave. "I was in your shoes once. The curriculum is important. It can make the difference between a dead agent and a live one. For some of us, though? The truly gifted of us? We need more than constant rules and regulations. Non-stop red tape. We came to do some good in the world, don't you agree?"

"I do, sir," she replied. "Yes."

"I'm here to offer you a job," Greene said. "The training will be more rigorous, the risks increased. The reward, however, is a chance to make a difference now, not after sitting behind a station desk for ten years."

"This isn't through the Bureau?"

"No," Greene answered. "This is outside the agency. Outside rules and regulations."

"I don't know what to say, sir," Metcalf said. What Greene offered was a chance to give her life meaning. Yet to do so outside the law and the purview of the country?

"I'm hoping for a yes." Greene stood up; his tall frame blocked the light from the window at his back. It threw his face into shadow, except for his large green eyes. "Anything else is a waste of my time and your talent. Say yes to your future."

Metcalf stood and extended her hand. "Sign me up, sir."

"Glad to hear it," Greene said. "I'll put the paperwork in motion. You'll be transferring to a new post."

Greene passed along the info. Metcalf glanced at the directives listed on the cover sheet. "Black Mesa?" she asked, confused. "I thought it was shut down years ago."

"It was."

"I'm not sure I understand, sir," Metcalf said. "Who will I be reporting to?"

"Me," Greene replied. "But in a different capacity. One far away from Washington and its endless debates. I built our group to aspire to be something more, something better."

Metcalf stared at her new assignment, and the potential within. "I look forward to doing my part, sir."

"Excellent," Greene said with a smile. "Welcome to the Trust, Metcalf."

CHAPTER SEVEN

Adler crawled through the tunnels behind the server wall. As the lowest point in the Bunker, fiber-optic cables and electrical wire filled the cavity that fed to every room and down every corridor throughout the entire complex.

There were no lights inside. The only beam that guided Adler's way was attached to the pair of glasses she wore. A small camera connected to the other lens, and fed her location to the only person willing — as well as capable — to help her in her mad search for the mysterious signal that had plagued her for weeks on end.

Nixon said nothing, yet she fully felt his presence at all times. Long breaths huffed through her earpiece. Grumbles of motion rang out from his shifting chair inside the server room. The door to the extensive server cavity remained open. When she turned back, Adler saw the man's sympathetic face. He went along with her plan, backed it up when brought to Kanigher — who became immediately lost when she began discussing the process. Nixon helped boil it down for the man, then signed on as an extra pair of hands.

Adler appreciated the gesture. Knowing Nixon believed in the plan gave Adler the confidence to move forward.

The signal had eluded her every effort. It had thwarted every attempt to pinpoint and trace its origins. No signal was that sophisticated. Nixon agreed. To get their internal systems up to snuff to track their elusive prey, they decided to reboot the system.

The signal specs taken from the Cove incident remained locked in the mainframe. Once rebooted, the system would prioritize the information pertaining to the signal, turbo charging the processors to focus on the signal and only on the signal.

Still, rebooting the mainframe came with its own risks. Electricity ran throughout the hidden nook. Some smaller areas were shut down for the procedure—the training room and certain storage closets—to minimize her risk of electrocution. Most of the systems, though, needed to continue running for their personal safety. It was part of the drawback of living underground. One of the main ones, right next to missing out on the floating ball of fire that showed up in the sky every day.

Carefully, Adler crossed the first threshold between wires. Sensitive to her surroundings, she made sure not to touch anything unnecessarily. Her cautious behavior, however, delayed the process. It wasn't apparent how slowly she had taken things until Nixon's sigh filled her ear. It wasn't the first occurrence since the start of her travels.

"Do you mind?" Adler asked through their shared comm link.

"Mind what?" Nixon said. She could hear keys clattering. He was always working on something, most likely devising a path through the data room for her, but for all she really knew, Nixon might have been playing *Galaga*.

"You keep sighing."

"Do I?"

"Repeatedly," Adler said. A heavy breath filled the line. "You just did it again."

"Sorry."

"You don't have to be here, Nixon." Adler shifted through the second threshold. She noted the terminal uplinks for communications, as well as their broadband hookup—something that definitely needed an upgrade when she found some downtime. "I appreciate you speaking on my behalf to Kanigher, though even that wasn't necessary."

"I like the glossed-over look in his eyes when you mention anything involving computers."

Adler chuckled. "It is the man's kryptonite."

"It brings me so much joy."

"I can tell," Adler said. "Seriously, though, I can figure this out."

The lie was not one of her best. Truthfully, she had moved far beyond her field of expertise. Tech girl was a nice line on the résumé, but for all intents and purposes, she only understood the basics compared to someone like Nixon. Zac, on the other hand, would have figured this signal issue out weeks ago. He was supposed to be here with the team, not her.

Adler pushed the thought away, angry at her inability to see things differently. She was with the DSA, not Zac. She had tried to bring him back to the fold. He'd resisted her efforts. It was time to handle things her way.

"No way," Nixon said. "I want to help. I'd be in there with you, if we could both fit in the womb together." A long silence filled the line. "That sounded weird, didn't it?"

Adler laughed. "Very much so." She shuffled around the first turn through the power conduit, feeding much of the private quarters. "Is this—"

"Yes," Nixon said. "You've got it."

"Good," Adler replied, and continued on her way. Heat filled the cramped space, causing the glasses to fog up intermittently. "I've run out of options, Nixon. The system can't grasp the signal. It's too slow to trace it to the source of the destination. This reboot has to work."

"And I agree completely," Nixon said. "It's the smart move."

"Not feeling like that to me right now," Adler commented. "I almost feel like I'm lost in space with how dark it is in here. Lost in an alien ship. Nothing looks right to me."

"That's how I feel out here."

Adler groaned. She had hoped to avoid the subject, another impossibility of late. "This isn't working, is it?"

"What do you mean?"

"I thought this would be a decent distraction," Adler answered. "But we're both skirting it the second there is a break in the conversation."

Nixon's typing ceased. "It is difficult not to ask. What do you think we should do with Susan?"

"I wish I knew."

"I mean, I know there's the whole lying thing to consider, but who doesn't hold back a thing or two now and then?"

Adler stopped her approach toward the next juncture. "Do you?"

"Me?" Nixon's voice cracked through the line. His nervousness brought a smile to her face. "That's beside the point."

"Seem pretty relevant right—"

Lights outside the room dimmed, then went out. Seconds ticked by, three passing quickly before they returned.

"What was that, Nixon?"

"A glitch."

"The lights—"

"I saw," Nixon interjected. The typing was back, more feverish than before. Nixon clearly didn't care for the surprise any more than she did. "Had to be a glitch. Probably from your tinkering."

"I haven't touched anything yet."

"That you know of," Nixon said. "Everything you brush by is extremely sensitive."

"I'll keep it in mind," Adler grumbled. "Just make sure I'm out of here before it happens again."

"I take it we're done discussing Susan, then?"

"Please." Adler didn't know what to think, or what to believe about the woman. Metcalf had brought her into the fold, and she appreciated the trust placed in her skills. Adler had never doubted the woman's leadership abilities until she'd met the Witness. He had a way of changing things, it seemed, and never for the better.

"Got it," Nixon said. "Where do we start?"

"How about the scanners?"

"All right. Take a left at the next junction."

Adler tucked away her doubts and her fears. She put aside the mistrust and the divisions that plagued her team. The signal was the key to bringing them back, to having everything make sense for all of them. This was going to work.

It had to.

CHAPTER EIGHT

They needed the break. The discussion might have continued for hours if not for Kanigher's suggestion. Ben accepted the reprieve, grateful for Kanigher's perspective on the proceedings. The talk became heated in Metcalf's absence. More and more, each member's voice raised in anger and frustration—none more so than Morgan's.

She continued to carry the tune through the Bunker during their timely intermission. "She's got to go."

Ben understood her point of view better than most. There had been too many secrets in his past, too many mysteries still to be solved, to be worried about those from their own colleague. The Witness stood at the center of them this time around. If only he hadn't given them the slip after their recent case in Colorado. They had even tracked the man back to the Millington facility, but by the time they had arrived, it was too late.

Flames had consumed the entire lumber mill. There had been no evidence left behind. All the clues to the Witness' next move had been scorched from the earth.

That had been the tipping point for most of the team. Ben read the room clearly on that front: the Witness was a threat, and Metcalf had been working with him for far longer than anyone knew about. Yet the enigmatic stranger continued to plague Ben's thoughts.

The Witness had saved Ben's life. He had injected a miracle drug into the dying man and removed all signs of injury. Not only had scrapes and bruises vanished, even gunshot wounds healed instantly. Ben had never felt more alive, or more frightened by the knowledge of his savior and the method used to rescue him.

For Morgan, the Witness' connection with Metcalf was more cut and dry. The Witness was a killer through and through. He was the reason for so much loss of late, and no amount of evidence to the contrary would prove otherwise.

"Did you hear me?" Morgan said. A steady pace carried her from the conference table, up the stairs, and toward the kitchen. "I said, she's got to—"

"I heard you the first twenty times, Morgan," Ben replied. He followed her slowly, hoping to avoid Morgan's wrath as much as possible.

"She's holding back, Ben." Morgan took a seat at the counter overlooking the stove.

From behind them, Kanigher returned from the dormitories with an empty tray. He headed behind the counter and jammed the dish in the sink to make room for the mounting pile left from the previous day. Both trailed Kanigher's movements through the kitchen as he collected spices and utensils for his next project.

"I know." Ben joined Morgan at the counter. "But what—"

"That means more secrets," Morgan interrupted. "God only knows if there's an end to them with her."

"You can't be serious, Morgan," Ben said. "We're talking about Metcalf here. The DSA has always been her show."

"Who says it has to stay that way?"

Ben nearly fell from the stool. His eyes widened in surprise. "What?"

"You heard me."

"She handpicked us," Ben said. "All of us. She brought us here for the work ahead. You'd throw that away?"

"Not at all," Morgan said with the slight shake of her head. She pointed toward the dormitories. "Just her. We need to stand united. The Trust. Thirteen. The Witness. These are known threats. Worrying about the serpent in the Bunker is not an option."

"I don't know." The DSA without Metcalf? She had saved him from a prison sentence. Without her, he might have met the end of a shank in the showers at Attica, or some other not-so nice penitentiary. The outcome would have been the same. Her connection with his father also clouded the issue. To Ben, nothing was as black and white as it seemed.

Kanigher clearly read Ben's misgivings. "How about we table it for now? I can make some food for everyone."

"Finally, an option I can get behind," Ben declared with a smile.

Morgan groaned, then stood. "We're not done talking about this."

"Continue it in the freezer," Kanigher said. "I need some chicken breasts for the main course."

Morgan started around the counter for the deep-set freezer stationed along the back wall. When she passed Kanigher, she stopped. Both waited for Ben to move.

"What?" he asked in confusion. "You need both of us for this dangerous mission?"

"If it gets you away from me for two minutes of silence?" Kanigher said with a nod. "Hell, yes."

Ben tapped along the counter. Standing, he joined Morgan as the pair made their way to the freezer. Ben grabbed the handle and yanked the door loose from the frame.

"Don't miss us too much."

Kanigher threw him a wave and headed to the pantry on the far side of the room for more supplies.

Ben waited for a witty retort, but none came. It irritated him when Kanigher failed to engage. Undeterred, Ben ushered Morgan ahead into the cold.

"After you, Agent Dunleavy."

Another groan left her before she slipped inside the freezer. Ben kept the door ajar slightly as they entered to keep the cold from escaping too much. He found it funny when the lessons of his youth, and the constant annoyance of his father, made their way into his daily life.

The freezer held enough food to survive multiple cataclysms. Wire racks that ran along each wall contained boxed goods, meats of various sundry, and more.

Morgan moved deeper into the cold, on the hunt for Kanigher's meal. "This is stupid."

"So is writing off one of our own," Ben said sharply. He failed to realize she had meant the search for some chicken breasts and regretted his tone when she stopped to throw him a thin glare.

"She knew the Witness, Ben!" she yelled. "The whole damn time!" At his retreat, Morgan paused and took a deep breath. Her hands fell to her sides. "You know what? Maybe Kanigher's right."

"That would be a first."

"A break," Morgan said. "Until after lunch."

"Good." His brow perked up, and his pace quickened at the sight of the chicken in question. He pulled a package from the rack. "I plan on savoring this, so it might be a while."

Morgan rolled her eyes. Goosebumps ran along her arms. She tried to wipe them away on her journey back to the door.

"Did you close the door?" she asked.

"What am I, an idiot?" Ben shook his head. "Don't answer that."

"Don't have to." Morgan pushed the handle to release the door. It didn't budge.

"Morgan?" Ben called, the chicken bitter cold against his palms. "Open the door."

"What does it look like I'm trying to do?"

Ben set the chicken down on an empty shelf. "Hilarious. Who knew you were such a comedian?"

Morgan backed away from the door, waving him ahead. "Try for yourself, muscle man."

Ben pushed the handle to no avail. He stepped back, then threw his entire body against the door to knock it from the frame. Concern filled him as the cold bit through his skin like knives.

"It's locked."

CHAPTER NINE

Zac had wanted nothing more than to see his wife since their separation. Every task he'd undertaken, every sacrifice he'd made, had been to earn her back. He'd washed dishes, slept in the grimiest of motels, and been on the run from various threats, all in the hopes of seeing her beautiful face once more.

This was not what he had in mind.

Claire stared at him from a distance. It had been over a minute since Hollis had tossed her inside for a reunion. That had been his term for it. Zac knew it to be nothing more than another threat. Hollis needed information about the Wellspring, and Zac's wife was now a bargaining chip to be used against him.

Despite the fear of knowing what lay outside the locked office, despite the terror of Hollis' threat against them, Zac couldn't help but smile at the sight of his wife. She was still his Claire, the mother of his only child, the woman who had kept him sane through college and in the years after. She held him together, kept him from losing touch with reality in his day-to-day life.

Zac held out his arms. "Claire."

She embraced him tightly. Tears streamed down her cheeks. "I missed you so much, Zac."

He pulled away to wipe her swollen cheeks. "But the divorce? The papers you mentioned on the phone?"

Claire shook her head, choking back her sadness. "I never went ahead with the lawyer. I…" She took a step away from him, concern filling her eyes. "Your face. What happened?"

Zac chuckled. "My face. My ribs. It's… It's a whole thing." The pain meant little to him with her in the room. He pulled her close once more. "I'm so sorry, Claire. This whole mess is my fault."

"Stop that, Zac," Claire replied. "I still love you, even after everything. I never stopped. I… Nothing has been right since our fight. Nothing has made sense at home."

Zac let her go. His hand slammed against his forehead. In his zeal to be reunited with his wife, he'd forgotten the missing element in their family's equation. Had it been the suddenness of the moment, or another sign of the Wellspring programming overwriting his brain? He feared the answer and focused on the return of the name at the tip of his tongue.

"Alex," he said. "Oh, God, was he—"

"He wasn't with me when they…" Claire trailed off. Her body shook at the thought of her abduction.

Zac cursed under his breath. He ran his hands over his face. She had been taken because of him. Every terrible act that had happened in her life stemmed from his own choices. "Hollis," he seethed. "I'll—"

Claire stopped him with a touch. Her fingers rested along his chest. Zac's heart quickened. "I'm okay," she said. "I am. But what do they want, Zac?"

His head bowed and his gaze fell to the floor. "Something I can't give them."

Zac turned away from her. He paced across the room, then leaned along the edge of the desk. Closing his eyes, Zac felt the presence tucked inside. This was about the Wellspring, and he was now that entity. He contained the knowledge of the previous incarnations, and though he fought against it, there was no stopping it.

Thoughts blitzed through his mind. The programming whispered to him in the voice of the deceased April Newton. He made no reply to the fast-paced insight offered by the centuries-old protocol. Instead, Zac grabbed the notepad and pen from the desk. He jotted down the details as they came, circling those deemed important as he went along. When he finished, Zac tucked the note in his pocket.

Claire's hand fell on his arm. She forced him away from the desk and back to her. "Zac?"

"I… I'm sorry, I—"

"I was talking to you," she said. "It was like you were in a different world."

Zac didn't know what to say, how to explain. Claire had taken the brunt of his behavior for too long. He had lived and breathed his job over his family for years. There was no more surprise in her face, only the same hurt he'd left her with weeks earlier.

"I'm sorry, Claire."

"This is about work, isn't it?" she asked. "More secrets. More lies."

"No." Zac took her hand and squeezed. "No, Claire, I wouldn't—"

Her hand fell away. She'd heard the excuses before, and they'd led to their separation. Zac didn't know how to make her understand what had happened, and what it meant for them.

In his silence, Claire's brow furrowed with anger. She pointed to the door. "If it isn't some secret, then just tell them what they want so we can go home."

"Home…" The word brought him such joy, yet it seemed farther away than ever. "It's… Everything I've done these past weeks has been to earn that right. It's all that keeps me going. All I want in this life."

She held out her hand for him. "Then let's go home. Please."

"I can't, Claire." He shook his head at the offer of her hand. "I can't give them what they want."

"Why?"

"This… This won't make much sense to you," Zac started. He paced the room, but stopped shy of the door. "That man out there? Hollis? He runs a group called the Trust. They control the world."

Claire grimaced. "What? Like in one of your comic books? Zac—"

His hand slammed against the wall. "This is real, dammit. This is happening. The Trust controls banks, tech firms, and media companies. They own the message. They craft innovations to push this country, and the world, toward a singular end."

"How?"

Zac lowered his voice. "Using someone called the Wellspring. A guide offering the future, but at a price."

"That's what he wants," Claire said. "This Wellspring. And you're protecting it."

"Her," Zac corrected. "Or it was a her. She died."

"Then who—"

Zac moved close to her. He stared deep into her eyes. The time for secrets was over, the time for lies long since past. There was only the truth left to share with the one person who mattered most to him.

"Me." At his admission, Claire reeled back a step. Confusion set in her face. Zac pressed ahead, keeping her close. "I'm the Wellspring. The knowledge is inside me, and I'm doing everything I can to keep it locked away. To keep it safe... from everyone."

The door opened behind them, and a jubilant Hollis stormed in. "Really?"

Fear filled Claire, who cowered at the back wall. It was the same fear Zac felt the second he realized what he had done.

"Oh, no."

Twin guards entered, weapons at the ready. Hollis, however, waved them down. He lorded his control over the situation with a devious smile.

"Well, now," he said with arms across his chest. "Isn't that interesting?"

CHAPTER TEN

Kanigher lined up the last of the spices next to the indoor grill. He checked over the list of supplies from the recipe to make sure everything matched what he'd found in the pantry. They definitely needed another supply run soon, the way he had been cooking of late.

Checking his watch, Kanigher noticed the minutes ticking by. "What the hell are they doing in there?"

Arguing was his first thought. It seemed to be their only shared passion. Morgan came from a more visceral approach, tackling her problems through conflict. She never wavered when confronted with a situation and always looked to plow straight to the heart of anything that stood in her path.

Ben's modus operandi, however, was rooted in passive aggressiveness. Arguing meant little to him. Ben merely enjoyed the verbal sparring, usually with a heavy dose of sarcasm thrown in for good measure. Kanigher certainly realized how deflated Ben appeared when silence was his only rebuttal. It brought a smile to Kanigher's face.

Arguing was only one option, though. Kanigher's mind took stock of the others. He passed the more adult scenarios fairly quickly: there was no way Ben could handle a woman like Morgan.

Patience at an end, Kanigher moved for the freezer door. He gripped the handle tightly and pulled. The door refused to budge.

"What the hell?"

He tried again with the same result. Banging on the door, Kanigher yelled, "Morgan? Ben? Everything all right in there?"

A stupid comment. The freezer door was locked tight. They sure as hell wouldn't be all right if that situation wasn't rectified. Kanigher started back through the kitchen. He slid to a halt at the sight of the Bunker entrance door, and a fearful thought struck him.

He raced over to try the door. With a calming breath, he pulled the handle. It failed to open. Gripping tight, Kanigher yanked the handle with all the strength in him. Nothing worked.

The lights above flickered. In a wave, the Operational Hub went dark. After a few seconds, the lights returned, and the monitors started up again. Kanigher jogged to the counter where he had placed his comm unit. Securing it in his ear, he tapped the line open.

"Nixon?" he called. "The lights keep fading, and the doors are—"

"Just a glitch in the system." Nixon sounded exasperated, as if he'd known the call was about to occur. The man's attitude frustrated Kanigher. "I'll be sure to look into it as soon as Alison is able to reset the system for her search."

They had mentioned the possibility of issues with the system. A power fluctuation or two, was what Kanigher had been told— nothing like what occurred all around him.

"Are you sure?" Kanigher pressed. "This seems more wide-spread than a single glitch. Maybe we should postpone Adler's work? Figure this out first. Ben and Morgan are—"

"There's absolutely nothing to be concerned about, Robert," Nixon said. He wasn't listening, Kanigher could tell through the blasé attitude over the line. Nixon preferred the work to people and, more importantly, Adler's work to that of the others. He saw it on the man's face during their previous mission and heard it clearly over the line.

"Nixon, this isn't—"

"Robert," Nixon interrupted. "It's a simple fix. I could do it in my sleep. There's nothing to—"

The lights went out again. The hum of electricity drained from the room. It didn't come in a wave this time, more like someone had flipped a switch for the entire place. Kanigher shuffled slowly through the thick black of the Operations area. He pried open the storage locker to the right of the entry door. Equipment clattered to the ground until he found what he'd been searching for. The click of a button brought a beam of white from the tip of the flashlight in his grasp.

Kanigher counted the seconds. When a minute had passed, he tapped the comm in his ear. "Nixon?"

"The lights are out there too, aren't they?"

"They are," Kanigher confirmed in a stern tone. "The exterior door is also locked."

"It is?" Nixon said in a high-pitch voice. "You're saying we can't get out of the Bunker?"

"That's what locked means."

"That doesn't make sense." Nixon rapped along his keyboard. The backlight on his screen must have provided enough illumination for him to continue working. "Why would that happen? Nothing Alison has been near would trigger that reaction. There's no—"

"You're rambling, Nixon," Kanigher said. "I take it I can be concerned now?"

"I would be, yes," Nixon replied with a gulp. "Deeply concerned."

CHAPTER ELEVEN

Vivian watched the drama unfold through the monitors. She sat, thrilled by every frantic movement picked up by the night-vision-capable cameras scattered throughout the Bunker. They were left on purposely, along with a few select systems, while all others crashed around the now trapped team of agents. Vivian wanted to capture every second of her revenge.

The man known as Kanigher scurried around Operations. He tried the freezer door once more, to no avail. Two of his colleagues remained trapped within, no camera to monitor their slow demise as the cold continued to surround them. *Too bad*, thought Vivian. They would be two more deaths whose blame rested with Metcalf. Their mere presence on her team confirmed their complicity.

Leaving Kanigher behind, Vivian shifted her attention to the mainframe. A lone tech worked with rising panic to figure out the reason behind the power failure. She didn't recognize him, but heard the name Nixon bellowed through their open communication line from an unseen colleague working behind the wall in the server room.

"Nixon?" the woman said, fear in her voice. "What's going on out there? I didn't touch anything, so what happened?"

"I don't know!" Nixon replied. He pounded at the keyboard, his diagnostics all failing, because his trust in Metcalf had been completely misplaced. "It isn't possible!"

That was the crux of the matter. They didn't know about the external control center. Metcalf hid that from them, as she did so much about her past. Vivian reveled in twisting the knife in their collective back. She would gladly show them all the truth behind their so-called leader.

Thinking of Metcalf, Vivian switched feeds again. All monitors in the control room changed to show the lone figure in her room. Bile caught in Vivian's throat at the sight of her, so much anguish and rage from a simple glimpse. Her hand rose to meet her dead eye, the pain a constant reminder of what she'd lost thanks to Metcalf's betrayal.

The woman offered no reaction. There was no fear in her face, no trepidation at the lack of lights. Metcalf sat at the end of her bed. She stared at the back of her door, waiting.

It was unacceptable. Vivian slammed her fist down on the console. The monitors shook, but the image remained clear. She wanted Metcalf to squirm, to understand true terror, like Vivian had for so long. It was the only way to grant her the end Metcalf deserved. And that end was coming.

Only then would Vivian be free from the torment of her past and the lives she had lost.

After her accident, and subsequent release from the hospital, she settled in northern Spain in a quaint village nestled near the coast. No recollection remained of her previous life; even her name had been lost to the incident that had taken her right eye. The nurse at the hospital had called her Nina, and it stuck with her.

Everything else came in time. Her comfort with the village, as well as the language, was something she worked to build through practice and patience. It was the latter where she struggled. Always quick to anger, her frustration got the better of her more often than not. Still, the lessons persisted until Nina found herself part of the community.

In the mornings, she took to the square for fresh fruits and vegetables. The market was always her favorite part of the village. Stands were set up around a large fountain, decorated with colorful foliage that ran to the park in all directions.

The people welcomed her as one of their own immediately. They offered her no pity for her injury, nor did they look down on her for her disability. Friendship and compassion surrounded the woman called Nina, and she found a home in the village.

Finishing up her daily shopping, Nina tucked the items into

the small bag she carried over her shoulder. One of her apples slipped loose. It rolled away from her, and she darted after the fruit frantically. When the shining red fruit slid to her right side, Nina lost sight of it for a moment. A curse rose to her lips; the injury still caused her grief after so long.

As she turned to grab the apple, Nina found it resting against the shoe of a well-dressed man. He wore sunglasses, a tan suit jacket, and a confident smile. Bending low, he retrieved the fruit.

"I take it this is yours?" he said in perfect English. It surprised her. The village predominantly spoke Spanish, and being away from most tourist attractions kept foreigners to a minimum. Nina, herself, was a rarity for the village, but she did as her neighbors had for her upon her arrival and welcomed the man with a gracious bow of her head.

"Thank you," she said. The words felt uncomfortable, though English remained her dominant language. "I appreciate the help."

The man handed her the apple, then glanced at her bag. "It looks like you have a full day ahead of you."

She laughed, noting the bottle of wine poking out next to the fruits and vegetables of her shopping. "A good book, and the beautiful weather. That's all I need."

"Are you sure?" he asked.

Her comfort level dropped. She took a step back, yet maintained her smile. "Positive. Have a wonderful day, and thank you again."

"You're very welcome."

The man's gaze followed her along the brick-laden path away from the park and down the street. Nina rounded the corner, a nervous grip along the strap of her bag. It wasn't just the man who took away her comfort, it was the sight of others on the street she failed to recognize.

She breathed easier the moment the door to her one-bedroom home closed behind her. The place wasn't much in the way of space, but the terrace out back overlooking the ocean was enough to keep her content. Nina removed the items from her bag and set them on her kitchen counter. Wine bottle in hand, she grabbed a glass and stepped outside. Her book waited on the small chair, and all thought of the encounter earlier vanished.

She lost the afternoon to the sunshine. The book kept her enthralled, and the wine kept her relaxed enough to never want the day to end. Nina stepped back into the home as the sun began to set in the distance.

Three men stood inside her kitchen. Two of them wore dark suits, their eyes obstructed by sunglasses. She recognized them from earlier in the square, as she did the third among them. He bit into an apple, the one he'd helped her retrieve.

"It's a beautiful home," he declared, as she closed the door to her small terrace.

"Who are you people?" Nina said. She tried to stand taller, tried to fight back the fear that came at their presence. "What are you doing in my home?"

"We… I've been looking for you," the man said. He set the apple down, then reached for a towel to clean his hand. "Nina, isn't it?"

"Why?"

The man ignored the question. He barely even looked at her, taking in the room. "That's not your real name, though. This home, this life, is not truly yours at all. Merely a replacement for what was stolen from you."

Nina's hand rose to her dead eye. How did he know so much about her? "Who are you?"

"You've lost so much," the man continued. "Your memory. Your eye. And time. So much time."

"Stop," Nina said when he approached her. "Stop, or I'll—"

The man stood before her, unafraid. His hand lifted her chin, raising her gaze to meet his own. "My name is David Hollis, and I've come to take you home. I'm here to offer you back your life."

It never felt that way to her, not in that moment and not now. Hollis' declaration stripped another life away from her. Piece by piece, the serenity of Nina broke apart and shattered like glass, and Vivian Ness was reborn. Both sides of her soul, however, remained shadows of their former selves.

She had lost the peace of the village with Hollis' arrival. The questions of what happened had taken over, and soon Vivian was back in the US, trying to piece together her former existence.

What she had found was emptiness waiting for her. There

had been no grand reunion, no great gathering of lost friends for her to reconnect with after so long. No, those connections had withered on the vine during her absence. The people she had once known and loved had moved on in her absence.

Vivian dangled on a precipice of loneliness and waited for the ledge to give way beneath her feet. Her entire life had been stripped from her.

It was the same feeling she wanted for Metcalf. Leaning toward the monitor, Vivian leered at the woman. She waited for the fear to take hold.

If it took the death of every single person in that bunker to make Metcalf's fear a reality, then so be it.

CHAPTER TWELVE

Something was wrong. The lights were still out.

Metcalf had prepared for its eventuality after learning about Adler's endeavor—and Nixon's involvement in the proceedings. Nixon was the definition of calamity, as noticed during his recent spell of "upgrading" the training arena. Why those lifelike automatons had truly been necessary was a question still waiting to be answered in her mind, though Metcalf had long since given up on the possibility of a rational explanation from Nixon. His tinkering was part of his process—how he worked through the larger issues the DSA presented him with—though Metcalf chalked up his behavior to his inability to rest like a normal person.

As the minutes continued to tick by, however, Metcalf realized something must have gone wrong during their reboot.

There were, of course, other rationales to explain the delay in the lights. Adler's poking around the mainframe might have caused an unexpected surge. Kanigher's use of the kitchen could have blown a fuse. Hell, for all Metcalf knew in her self-imposed exile, Ben might have plugged his hair dryer in the same outlet as his space heater.

Part of her wanted to go out and ask. That instinct carried throughout her body and leaked out through her fingers as they tapped along the baseboard of her bed. Surely if there was an issue, someone would tell her, wouldn't they?

The answer startled her. The truth was self-evident just from the silence permeating the room. They didn't need her involvement. More than that, they didn't want it. Any interference from Metcalf would only come across as a need to take control of the situation.

Metcalf refused to fall into that trap. She flat out denied any need to step outside her room, only to learn the problem had been handled. The others could deal with anything. She had recruited them in the first place for that reason. Plus, Metcalf hated the idea of Morgan finding out about her concern over their affairs. No doubt Morgan would throw it right back in Metcalf's face—just another sign of Metcalf's mistrust of the team when this was anything but.

"Dammit," she grumbled under her breath. This was exactly what she hoped to avoid. Their latest intervention, their unexpected tribunal over her behavior, left Metcalf questioning everything. That wasn't what the team needed right now. The mission remained the same, and it was time to get back to it before something catastrophic—and completely preventable— occurred.

Metcalf held her tongue. One minute, then another, passed without resolution. Finally, she couldn't take anymore and pushed off the bed. Heading to the door, Metcalf hesitated only for an instant before stepping outside.

Darkness ran the length of the corridor. She saw no light around the corners. The entire place appeared to be in the same boat. It was an impossibility. Multiple redundancies were in place to prevent such a situation. Her first thought repeated in her mind:

Something is wrong. Very wrong.

Metcalf ran her hand along the wall beside the door. A small latch caught her finger, and she held firm. Shifting closer, she edged the latch open to reveal a panel within. Her eyes tried to adjust to the darkness without success. Using touch, Metcalf checked the wire connections within to see if there was a disconnect to the larger system. It didn't amount to much in the way of a solution, but she couldn't think of anything else at the moment.

"What the hell are you doing?" A bright light cut through the shadows and fell on her position. She pulled away from the wiring terminal to shield her eyes. A massive figure stepped closer, but the flashlight made it impossible to see them clearly. Good thing she recognized the voice immediately.

"Bobby?"

He lowered the flashlight, but kept it on to offer them something in the way of illumination. Metcalf lowered the hand from her eyes, only to find Kanigher's coming at her. He crossed his forearm over her clavicle and pushed her into the wall.

"Bobby!"

"What did you do?" Kanigher said. "What's going on?"

"I…" Metcalf fought for words. She had known the man for years, yet had never seen him so direct. Fury overtook him, and he aimed every ounce toward her. "What?"

"The entire complex is out right now." With each word, his arm jammed tighter against her. "The only way out of this underground box is locked. Our people are trapped in the damn freezer, and you're walking around pulling at wires. Did you do this?"

His words stung. Her hands fell on his arm. "Bobby, I… I didn't do this. You have to—"

"Don't."

It was the wrong thing to say. Today, of all days, it was absolutely the worst thing to say to the man. Her head bowed, and her gaze softened. "You're right. You don't have to trust me, but try to believe me when I say this wasn't me."

Kanigher read her face. He was so close, Metcalf felt the heat rising from him. His concern for the others was palpable, yet hers remained with him, and how he'd reacted to her innocence.

His arm fell away, and Kanigher took a step back. "Good."

He glanced up and down the hallway, letting the flashlight lead the way. Nothing was in sight, but that meant little to them. If there was a threat, it was here, and they had to find it.

"Ben and Morgan?"

"I can't get to them," Kanigher said. "The door is jammed. Same as the exterior door."

"There are redundancies in place to keep that from happening." She headed back into her room. Reaching under her pillow, she pulled her Glock free. She released the clip, verified it was full, then jammed it back into place.

"Nixon said the same thing."

"And is he—"

"He's looking into it," Kanigher replied. "According to him, though, all our internal systems were tied up with Adler's pet project."

"Giving someone the perfect opportunity to hit us."

"But who?"

"I wish I knew," Metcalf said. She caught the glare from her companion. "Bobby…"

"Sorry," he said, waving down the argument. "Reflex."

"Nixon give a timetable on how long to get us back up and running?"

"All he would say is, he's working on it with Adler," Kanigher answered. "It didn't sound like it would be soon."

"Great."

Metcalf moved for the corridor once more. Kanigher held her up, a gentle hand along her forearm.

"How could something like this happen, Susan? If it didn't come from the internal systems, who could access the Bunker from outside?"

"I—"

"I could, Agent Kanigher," a voice through the comm system said. Her words boomed through the small room. Metcalf and Kanigher spun toward the camera positioned in the corner. "And I did. All so I could pay back the woman who stole my life from me."

CHAPTER THIRTEEN

Hollis had heard every word. Zac's astonishment kept him locked in position, a statue in the center of the room. Claire's horror sent her reeling for the back wall, where he should have been. That was his role, the job he'd been dreaming of since losing her: that of Claire's protector.

It was foolish to reveal the truth to his wife. His admission had done more to harm their chances than any lie would have. Hollis played on Zac's need to be with his wife with complete and total success. Now, they found themselves trapped with the head of the Trust. His two guards blocked the only door to the room. Hollis held all the cards, and no solution screamed in Zac's brain.

There was only the pain of silence.

"Wait!" Zac shouted at Hollis' approach. A hand broke from his statue-esque stance, barring Hollis from Claire. Hollis cared little and continued toward Zac with a zealous grin. "Don't!"

Hollis grabbed Zac by the collar. He lifted him from the ground, then shoved him against the wall. "You were holding out on me, Zac."

"You're wrong," Zac lied. "I—"

"Please," Hollis spat in his face. "If you didn't think this room was bugged, you're not quite the intellect I imagined."

"Leave him alone!" Claire rushed to Zac's rescue. Her hands acted like sledgehammers against Hollis' back. They did nothing against the man. When the guards moved to intercept her, Hollis shook his head.

"Enough," Hollis snapped. He dropped Zac to the floor. An elbow shot out and clipped Claire across the chin. The blow drove her back. Hollis loomed over Zac. "So the old woman didn't make it out of the Cove and left you holding the bag?"

"I…"

Hollis snatched Claire's arm. He pulled her close, and his hand seized her throat. "No more lies, Zac."

"Okay, okay." Zac made his way to his feet slowly. "You're right. It's true."

"Prove it." Hollis' grip tightened around Claire's throat. "Prove it quickly."

"I don't know how." His mind reeled for some way to answer. Closing his eyes, Zac begged for the voice in his head to speak—to save the day as she had multiple times during their time together. Nothing came, not in a whisper or even an argument. The quiet spoke volumes about the threat Hollis truly posed. "Hollis, listen to me…"

"I'm trying, Zac," Hollis said. "You're just not saying anything of interest." Claire choked from the man's grip. Her hands dug into Hollis' without success. "Tick, tock."

"Wait," Zac said. "What about the car engine? I built it in Grand Island. It's still in my motel room."

"We're well aware."

Zac lost two days to the engine's construction. The project consumed his entire consciousness, bleeding out from the Wellspring. All of his fighting caused the programming to take over, like the thought itself demanded release from within his brain.

The engine held no carbon footprint. The concept of a clean engine would not only change the automotive industry but the entire planet, yet when mentioned to Hollis, the only response was a glower.

"You developed a similar concept when you were twelve, Zac," Hollis said. "I've read your file enough to know your brilliance at work. I'll need something more from you."

"I don't have anything more!"

Hollis leaned close to Claire's ear. "Guess he doesn't really love you after all, my dear."

"Wait!" Zac screamed. "Please! Wait. I can—"

Pain shot through his head. Zac crumbled from the agony; his body collapsed against the carpet. His hands shot to his temples, squeezing tight to his skull to stem the sensation.

"What is this now?" Hollis' question sounded distant, as if

part of another room in a different building, instead of directly above Zac.

Zac shut his eyes and found April waiting for him inside his mind. She appeared sickly, weakened from the extended connection. Her withered frame circled him, a look of condemnation on her face.

"Don't do this, Zac," April said. "This is a mistake."

"Then help me," Zac pleaded. He couldn't stand; the pain kept him on the metaphysical ground as much as the reality that awaited him. "Give me something to offer Hollis."

"You can't offer that man anything."

"He has my wife!"

She offered no sympathy, only the cold calculation of the threat. "One life doesn't compare to the billions at risk if Hollis reacquires the Wellspring."

"You spent years working for him!" Zac bellowed over the throbbing of his mind. "Why?"

"There were no other options," April said. "The programming took precedence. You don't have to give in. You don't have to serve the grand purpose. Not yet. Not if you—"

"That's it, isn't it?"

Realization washed over April. "You can't be serious."

"He doesn't know about it, does he?" The pain diminished with the new thought raging in his mind. April's presence faded.

"You can't offer that to him," April said. "Not for anything in the world. Not even Claire."

"I don't have a choice."

Claire's life was at stake. If there was a way to save her, to give them a second chance, then he had to take it.

Zac's eyes snapped open. His body relaxed, the pain gone for the moment. He remained on the carpet staring up at a waiting, and thoroughly confused, Hollis.

"A nice ploy, Zac," Hollis said, Claire still in front of him. "But your little fit gives you nothing. Not if you don't give me something right now."

Only one card remained to play. April's desperate pleas fell silent in the background. Zac stood before Hollis, locking eyes with the man.

"The signal," Zac said. "I can lead you to the signal."

"What signal?"

He didn't know. April had kept it hidden from him, just as she'd attempted with Zac. "One hidden outside the usual bandwidth. One relaying terabytes of information constantly for download and distribution via the Wellspring Protocol."

Hollis' grip relaxed along Claire's throat. She immediately pulled away and her hands latched to the edge of the desk for support. She fought for breath. Zac wanted to help her, but was cut off by an enraptured Hollis.

"I knew it," he said. "She was never the source of the information. All those ideas? Someone was feeding her the knowledge."

Zac nodded to confirm.

The awed smile faded from Hollis' face, and his eyes thinned. "Where is it?"

"No."

"Zac," Hollis intoned. His hands balled into fists, prepared for another strike. "This is no time to hold out."

"I tell you, and we're both dead."

The guards at the door shifted their weight uncomfortably. Both reached for the guns at their sides. Hollis waited for the movement to stop, the threat clear enough for Zac.

"You don't, and what do you think happens?"

"I know exactly what happens." Zac's lip curled. He leaned close to Hollis. "You never get your answers."

The reply staggered Hollis. Zac took the moment of silence to check on Claire. Fear caused her body to shake at his approach. Sadness filled her upon realizing it was her husband by her side and not the others in the room.

His own sadness matched hers. This wasn't what he wanted, wasn't what he'd envisioned all those weeks away from each other.

"Are you okay?" he asked quietly.

Claire tried to nod, her hand grazing her bruised throat. "Yeah, but…"

"I love you," Zac said.

"I love you."

Hollis grumbled at Zac's back. The concerned husband turned away from the love of his life to face their captor once more. "I'll take you there, Hollis. You let Claire go, and I'll take you to the signal."

Hollis shook his head. "She comes with us."

"No," Zac replied. "That's not going to happen."

"You have my word, Zac." Hollis held a hand over his heart. "Your darling wife will be released as soon as we arrive at our destination. That is the deal. The only deal I am willing to offer, and the only one you will accept."

The truth rested in Hollis' eyes and resounded with every word spoken. Once Zac escorted the man to Bismarck—to the source of the signal—both Zac and Claire were dead. Hollis was correct, though. No other choice presented itself. To save Claire, Zac required time to think… and to plan.

Zac held out his hand. "Deal."

CHAPTER FOURTEEN

Ben struggled against the freezer door. He pushed against the handle, throwing his whole body into the affair. When that failed, Ben slammed his hands against the door. The cold stung his palms as he yelled, "Hey! We're in here!"

He heard nothing from the outside. No matter the pattern of knocks he pounded against the door, no reply arrived with the corresponding answer. How the hell it worked in every television show he'd ever seen, and every book he'd read, he didn't know, but he demanded his money back for the false advertising.

"Come on!" he shouted. "Someone open the damn door!"

He leaped at the door. Punching at the handle, Ben threw the entirety of his body into releasing the door from the frame. Instead, he flew back and crashed to the ground in a heap.

"Dammit," he muttered. Breath floated before his face. Whatever had jammed the door mechanism must have been specific since the cold continued to blast throughout the unit. Slow to stand, Ben kept his eyes locked on the door. "Let us out of here!"

"Please stop yelling for five seconds."

Morgan sat on a makeshift bench of boxed meals. Her legs tucked in close, her hands planted over her ears.

Ben kicked at the ground, then turned away from the door. "How can they not hear us?"

"We've been taking classes on tuning you out," Morgan said.

"Really?" Ben shot back, incredulous. "Right now with the jokes?"

Morgan shrugged. Her hands fell from her ears. She wrapped her arms tight across her chest, shivering. Tilting her head to the door, she said, "You carrying?"

Ben raised an eyebrow at the question. "For a freezer run?" He patted his pants dramatically. "No. I forgot to strap on my Ruger to tackle this dangerous mission."

Morgan grimaced. "Bullet probably would have ricocheted off the door, anyway."

"And hit me, no doubt," Ben said with a smile.

"I'm too pretty to die in a freezer," Morgan replied. Her lip curled.

Ben joined her on the bench. "I always forget that."

Morgan's hand shot out and punched him in the arm playfully. "Watch it, Riley."

Ben rubbed at the impact site with a wry smirk. "Ow."

Silence fell between them. The cold made it difficult to focus, but both stared off toward the door. Something was wrong outside, something worse than either could imagine, though Ben did the best he could with what little information he gleaned from their current predicament.

Taking out half of the agents in the place at such an opportune time required careful planning. Ben hated that Kanigher came to mind immediately. His own experience with the former-NSA agent before he'd joined their team had been less than ideal. Kanigher had been one of a pair of agents sent to bring Ben in for questioning. At the time, Kanigher had seemed loyal to Stallworth and Sullivan.

Had it truly been a ruse all along? Ben had a difficult time believing such a masterful act by the straight-laced agent. Yet, if he had planned their entrapment in the freezer, what was his endgame? Stallworth had been taken into custody. Sullivan was gone, presumed dead.

"Do you think Kanigher—"

Morgan spoke over his theory. "Do you think Metcalf—"

Both stopped. Morgan's train of thought had taken her in a completely different direction, but with the same result. Their lack of trust, the divisions that had formed in the team thanks to Metcalf's secrets, continued to grow. At the sound of Morgan's working theory, Ben tucked his own away.

"You think Metcalf did this?" Ben scoffed. "Really?"

"Says the man willing to blame Kanigher."

"He worked for Stallworth."

Morgan stood. "He was going to make you lunch! Does that sound like the grand plan of some master criminal?"

"Metcalf—"

"Don't," Morgan snapped. "Don't defend her again, Ben. Please."

Morgan settled back on the seat next to him. Ben shifted closer; their shared body heat helped battle back the cold to some extent. Both were right in their own way. Both hated the way it felt to give their theories a voice, however.

Ben ran his hands over his face. He tried to push through the doubts brought up lately, then sighed at his inability to do so. His hands fell away, and he turned to face Morgan, who continued to stew.

"We have to talk about her, don't we?" Ben said.

"Ben..." The anger crept into Morgan's voice.

"Maybe it's not Metcalf."

"What do you mean?" Morgan asked. "For this?"

Ben shook his head. "No. Well, I mean, I don't think she'd do this. What I'm trying to talk about is..."

"Take your time."

He leaned forward. "Listen for a second, Morgan. I've been mulling it over since I almost... Well, the whole dying thing has that effect on people, I guess."

"Ben?"

"What I'm trying to say is, what if it's the DSA that's the problem?" The question threw her for a loop. Morgan opened her mouth to respond. Ben cut her off. "What if it's all of this, all of us, that's the issue? Maybe it all needs to go away."

"What?" Morgan exclaimed. "End it? After everything we've seen? Everything we've been fighting for?"

Ben jumped to his feet. "And what good have we really done? What difference have we made, Morgan?" Ben thought of Emily Wright. His former partner was just the tip of the iceberg when it came to their failures—to his failures. "What if we're merely obscuring the landscape with our good intentions? Maybe there are other people who can do it better."

Morgan's voice softened. There was no more anger. Only sadness remained. "Maybe no one else will try."

"They might be right not to, Morgan," Ben said. "The fact is, we don't know, even after everything, if we're on the right side of this. Do we?"

Morgan offered no answer. The room grew colder at the silence.

CHAPTER FIFTEEN

"You left me for dead," the voice said through the open comm link. "I may as well have been. I lost my life, everything I ever knew, because of what you did to me."

Metcalf heard the woman's every word. She tried to analyze it, to parse every syllable for clues as to the woman's identity. It tickled Metcalf's memory, but recognition failed.

Kanigher leaned close. "Do you—"

"No," Metcalf interrupted.

"Why would you?" the woman's voice boomed. She had tried to remain calm and collected previously. She controlled the situation completely, yet rage crept through her words. "I was just another one of your victims. You saw me as nothing but an obstacle in your path. Like so many others. You've seen it, Agent Kanigher. You know exactly who Susan Metcalf is, don't you?"

Metcalf's hands balled into fists at her sides. Enough accusations had been laid at her feet over the course of the day, the week, even this lifetime. To be fed more by some faceless attacker went too far. She moved closer to the camera, fury ready to be unleashed.

Kanigher stopped her with a hand on her shoulder. He cut her off from view. "You're right. I know her."

"Bobby…"

Kanigher shook his head, his eyes on the camera. "She's made mistakes. We all have."

"There is no justifying what she did to me," the voice spat.

"Maybe," Kanigher said. "But we won't know that unless we can talk things out. Now, there are people down here who have done nothing to you. Let them go, and we can have that talk."

"No." The anger was gone. The rage had been an error, and one quickly corrected. The voice was in full control of the situation and knew it well. "There will be no talking. No negotiations. No last-minute rescues. I've planned this for too long, worked too hard not to see this through."

"Now listen—" It was Metcalf's turn to stop Kanigher. His eyes fell on her. Even through the darkness that surrounded her, she spotted the sadness in them. "Susan, there has to be a way out of here."

Metcalf's gaze lowered, and she stepped away from the man. Her mind whirled with options, contingencies that amounted to nothing more than additional secrets kept from the others. Her arms crossed her chest tight, like a comfortable blanket. No matter the options, something continued to nag at her: the voice with no name. Metcalf tried to place her, tried to identify her words from the myriad victims of her past. There was only one way to make that happen.

"Tell us."

"Susan, what are you doing?" Kanigher asked.

"She's building up to her ultimatum, Bobby." Metcalf pointed to the camera. "I want to hear it."

"Very well," the voice replied. "The exit is now unlocked. You will take the elevator topside. Metcalf, and only Metcalf, will take the elevator, Agent Kanigher. There will be no gimmicks, no tricks, and absolutely no interference from your so-called team. This ends today."

"Wait one second," Kanigher snapped. "That's not—"

"You have ten minutes," the voice said. "The clock starts now."

"That's not going to happen," Kanigher said. "Not a chance in hell. You want her, you have to go through me."

"That's not necessary, Bobby."

"What?" Kanigher spun toward her. "We don't know who this is. We don't know why she wants you."

"I can certainly guess." Metcalf peered through him to the dim light of the camera lens. "He's right, though. Why me?"

Whatever had been done to the woman on the other end of the comm had left her broken and in pain. Rage had been her only response, seen through her actions and heard through her words. Silence allowed the woman to maintain her control. It kept her in charge, but offered Metcalf nothing in the way of answers.

Metcalf tired of not having any answers.

"You want me? That's the price," Metcalf yelled into the line. "I want the details. I know I'm a bitch. I've heard it quite a few times today alone, so why don't you tell me what I've done to deserve your wrath?"

Metcalf's chest heaved. All her frustration slipped from her, and she tried to rein it in. She had wronged everyone in her life, this life she had spent so long meticulously building. In the course of a few days, her team — those closest to her — had turned on her. They demanded answers to questions they could barely fathom. Then there was this woman, another one wronged by Metcalf, another who demanded her pound of flesh. Who were they to ask such things of her? Who were any of them to deem Metcalf the villain of the story?

When the voice returned, the answer became apparent to Metcalf. True villains lived in the world, and for the woman at the other end of the line, Metcalf sure as hell fit the role in her story. All it took was one word from the voice to bring recognition.

"Madrid."

All doubt about the voice's identity left Metcalf. There was also no question what would happen to the other members of Metcalf's team if she didn't follow the woman's instructions to the letter.

Kanigher, however, looked to Metcalf for an answer. "Susan? What the hell does that mean? You've never been to Madrid, have you?"

"Yeah, Bobby, I have." Metcalf stared up at the darkness of the camera. "Once."

CHAPTER SIXTEEN
Ten Years Ago

The sun scorched her skin. Even through the baseball cap she wore, Metcalf felt the heat threatening to singe her scalp. A haze from the midday sun rose along the horizon, the cityscape lost behind a wave of trees on the edge of the Parque de la Montaña.

Madrid was home to many such places, tucked away from the thoroughfares of the city—hidden treasures one had to hunt for in order to view. The Temple of Debod was no exception. The transplanted Egyptian temple typically held a crowd of tourists throughout the day. Thanks to the recent construction surrounding the weathered temple, it lay vacant of viewers, and the park had been cleared of visitors.

Her team chose the site for this privacy. The multiple points of egress, with only one clear line of entry from the north side of the park, made it ideal for their needs.

Metcalf paced the perimeter. The waiting made her uneasy. The buyers were late, but that was merely the start of her issues with the mission. She didn't exactly know their entire objective, and that raised her anxiety to new levels. The package, the payoff, the buyers themselves, all remained shrouded from her.

Her assignment to the team had come late in the game. Greene had called her in from a scouting mission outside Muncie. A scientist of some renown had been making waves with his theories in nanotech and viral agents. The Trust had sent her to gain access to the scientist's inner circle, establish a connection with the man, then see if he would be worth recruiting to the Trust. If not, they had instructed Metcalf to take him out of the picture.

She had been on several missions like that over the years. She had grown comfortable with the scenario: winning someone over, learning their entire life, then playing the role of judge and executioner. Yet, this had been the first time she'd been forced to abort right before she'd infiltrated the man's lab. Metcalf had made a mental note to get back to Oliver Blake when time allowed.

The importance of the Madrid operation was immediately made apparent by Greene. It was vital to the Trust, and the future of the world. One member of the team had already been killed procuring the payoff for the package. Again, details never came up during her impromptu briefing, which had been relegated to a phone call instead of face-to-face.

More than anything about the mission—more than the lack of intel and the suddenness of her reassignment—Metcalf hated not being in command. A woman named Vivian Ness held that role. The strong-willed and determined woman worked for the CIA, or so her credentials claimed at any rate. She stood between the stone archways at the heart of the cobblestone path surrounding the temple. Vivian had set up a table with a lone item resting upon its surface: a briefcase. She kept a hand on the briefcase, unwilling—or simply afraid—to let go of it for a micro-second.

Vivian's team consisted of three members from Army Intelligence. They were from General Adams' camp. Metcalf had had enough run-ins with them to know them by name. William Dent, Nate Fremont, and Devon Byrne. On the job, they were consummate professionals. After hours, they were scumbags of the highest order. She had broken more than their hearts during their time together running jobs for the Trust. They each wore Kevlar vests and carried automatics hung over their shoulders. They came for war, a clear sign of the stakes involved.

"Metcalf," From her position, Vivian waved the pacing agent over. "A word."

Metcalf ended her latest circuit around the wide stone path and headed through the serpent-topped gateway for the table on the other side. "What's up?"

Vivian winced at the lack of protocol. "I need to know your head is in the game, Metcalf. I've been running ops for Greene through the CIA for years. This is the big leagues, and you're the only unknown on the field right now.

"Greene called me in." Metcalf stood up taller, offended at the accusation. "You have a problem with his decision?"

"I don't like questions I can't answer," Vivian said. She was a woman after Metcalf's own heart. Maybe that was why Metcalf disliked her so much. "I've worked with these boys before. They vouched for you. So did Greene. We get through this, there won't be a doubt in my mind who you are, and what mission you serve."

"No, there won't," Metcalf confirmed.

Vivian smirked at her arrogance. She cocked her head to the double-wide glass doors that led to the transplanted structure. "I need you to take up position at the temple's main entrance."

"I can be more use up front," Metcalf replied. "You might need someone for the long shot should this go sideways."

"It won't go sideways." Vivian's words were sharp. "Take your position, as instructed."

"Yes, ma'am," Metcalf said with a sarcastic salute. "Care to share what's in the case? Or what we're doing here?"

"A trade." Vivian swept her hair back and tied it off. Her green eyes sparked like emeralds. "They have something Greene wants."

"He didn't tell you either, did he?"

Vivian turned back to the road, no longer willing to engage with Metcalf. "Take your position."

Nate lowered his binoculars and turned from in front of the stone gateway at the edge of the road. "We've got incoming."

"Get ready, people," Vivian yelled to the others.

Two black sedans cut across the maintenance road to the outskirts of the site. They parked facing the archways, and the doors on all sides opened in unison as if planned for dramatic effect. Metcalf took her position at the entrance of the temple. She scanned each player as they arrived.

The sedans carried four men in each. Most wore leather jackets, gold chains around their necks, and sunglasses. Two, one from each car, wore purple robes with a clerical collar positioned around their necks. Every member of the approaching crew carried the same tattoo: black angelic wings scorched at the tips.

Metcalf had read about them before. They were known as the Order of the Fallen. All reports described them as a terrorist organization. Some labeled them as religious zealots with ties to the Catholic Church, but officials denied such a connection existed.

The typical lore surrounded the Order. There was talk about the Second Coming. Most of their actions, however, centered on the Book of Revelations and humanity's impending downfall. Either way, they were sadistic killers dressed as saints. Vivian's entire team tightened up at their approach, the numbers stacked against them.

"Are you in charge?" one priest asked. He had beady eyes and bony fingers.

"I am," Vivian answered. Her hand continued to hold tight to the briefcase handle.

"You have what's been asked?"

Vivian spun the case around. All eight members of the Order took a step forward, then stopped at the priest's rising hand. He continued to the makeshift altar in the center of the arches alone. Vivian opened the case; the lid of the briefcase obscured Metcalf's field of view. Metcalf shifted to the side for a better look, a hand always on her sidearm.

Inside was a laptop with a secure Sat-link connection. Vivian removed a small drive from the side to show her buyer. Pleased with the presentation, the man waved her on. Vivian slipped the drive back into place.

Metcalf continued her circuit of the stone walkway. It went against orders, but she needed to see what was being offered to the fanatical group. She nearly gasped when she recognized the information on full display.

The screen listed covert operations from every major American and European government organization. Not only were the major theaters for each mission displayed, but also every asset in the field. Their cover identities, personal information, as well as any relevant safe house and friendly in the area were offered on a silver platter to the priest and his men.

The priest reached for the case. Vivian snapped it shut in front of him, causing all to jump back a step.

"Our package?" she asked.

The beady-eyed man snapped his fingers. A thug in tight leather returned to the sedan. From inside, he retrieved the prize Vivian and her crew had been sent to retrieve.

Metcalf believed the package to be an item of great importance. She imagined it to be a relic, or piece of technology, that Greene sought from these terrorists. Instead, the thug removed an old woman from the back of the sedan.

"Enjoy it," the priest said with a thin smirk.

"It?" Metcalf's question echoed in the open space. Shocked stares shot her way, both from the opposition and her own team. Metcalf, however, continued to watch the woman. She fell to her knees on the road, her eyes blindfolded and her hands bound. "That's a person."

"That's enough, Agent," Vivian snapped.

Metcalf shook her head. "Are you kidding? We were brought here for intelligence retrieval. Some technology that—"

"And here it is," the priest interrupted. "Are we going to have a problem?"

"No." Vivian snapped up the briefcase with the covert information and lifted it from the table. "No problem at all. Right, Agent?"

Metcalf stared at the broken woman in the dust. She felt the weight of the briefcase even from across the walk. The information inside, in the hands of the Order of the Fallen, would result in hundreds dead. Thousands of lives would be thrown into turmoil at the loss of the covert assets in the field. Their work was more important than anyone realized.

"No," she said. "None at all."

The gun was in her hand before anyone could react. She knew their every position, tracked their movements and shifts in weight during the entire exchange.

Metcalf took out her own team first. Devon, Nate, and Will fell seconds apart from each other. Headshots ended their lives without a single chance of retaliation.

The priest's eyes cried out in panic. He fled for the road and the still-running sedans. Two shots to the back sent him to the ground with a thud. Shots erupted from the Order. Metcalf ducked behind the archway at her side, letting it absorb the rage from the thugs. Her clip fell to the ground, a replacement in position and ready for the next round.

A deep breath cleansed her. Metcalf stepped clear. Shot after shot hit their mark. For all their so-called preparation, the members of the Order considered no risk to their lives. They clearly believed in their numbers. Metcalf mowed them down. There was no remorse in the act. She didn't stop until dead men littered the ground.

"No!" Vivian screamed. She slammed the briefcase to the table. "What have you done?"

"What I had to." The gun recoiled, a lone shot cut across the wide gulf between them. The bullet pierced Vivian's right eye. Her head snapped back and slammed into the corner of the stone gateway as she fell to the ground. Metcalf stared at the surrounding dead. "I did what I had to."

Metcalf gathered up the briefcase. Quickly, she made her way to the still-kneeling woman in the dirt. She shook with fear, terrified to move. Metcalf removed the blindfold and cut her bindings.

"Are you okay?"

The woman looked around in awe. "You… You killed them."

"There was no other choice." Metcalf helped the woman to her feet. "We need to get you as far away from here as possible."

"They'll find me," she said. "They always do."

"I'll do what I can to help, but we need to leave now." Metcalf shuffled her to the passenger side of the sedan and helped her to the seat. She moved to close the door, when the woman's hand blocked her.

"Wait," she said. "I… I don't even know your name."

"Susan Metcalf. And you are?"

"April," the woman said with wide eyes. "April Newton."

CHAPTER SEVENTEEN

Metcalf recalled it all. She felt the heat on her skin, the blazing sun overhead through the hazy clouds, and the breeze that did little more than cause her shirt to cling to her sweat-soaked skin. She heard the bullets leaving her weapon, and the crashing of bodies to the dirt.

There had been no survivors other than Metcalf and April Newton—the woman at the center of so much tragedy: the woman Metcalf now knew to be the Wellspring.

Somehow, Metcalf had been wrong. Not about the mission, that she knew without a doubt to be the right thing to do. Saving April from the Trust—from Greene's clutches—was the only thing that truly mattered that day so long ago.

No, Metcalf had merely been wrong about the end results of her actions. The Trust had been willing to sabotage the safety of their top agents around the world for the sake of a single woman. Killing those involved was expedient. It was the efficient way of doing business.

Yet, Vivian Ness had survived.

Metcalf stood in the shadow of her private chambers, reliving every moment of that fateful day. Everything changed for her after Madrid, as assuredly as when Kenneth Riley had found her in the cage. Vivian, however, continued to live in that day. To her, Metcalf earned her wrath for the betrayal she had brought against Vivian and the rest of her team at the Temple of Debod.

Metcalf failed to disagree with the woman's sentiment. "I'll do it."

"What?" Kanigher staggered back a step with disbelief. Wide eyes greeted her. "You can't be serious. You can't—"

"I'm going up," Metcalf interrupted. She started for the door.

"Ten minutes," Vivian said through the comm. "Better get moving."

Kanigher skirted by her. He grabbed at the frame of the door, then filled the width to bar her path. "Stop!"

"Move aside, Bobby."

"Not a chance in hell."

Metcalf smirked at the challenge thrown her way. She plowed at him, intent on knocking him aside to squeeze through the gap. A sharp jab into his side might have been enough. Unfortunately, Kanigher anticipated the attempt. He took both arms in hand and pushed her deeper into the room.

"Let me go!" Metcalf yelled.

Kanigher tossed her to the bed. "Not until you tell me what the hell just happened here. She says Madrid, and you fold like a deck of cards? Who is this woman?"

Metcalf caught herself on the edge of the bed. Her hands clung tight to the footboard, her body dangling off the mattress and over the side.

"It doesn't matter."

"It does to me," Kanigher snapped. "So cut the crap, and tell me what I need to know."

It wasn't just a need, Metcalf thought, it was what Kanigher deserved to know. Over the years, he had put up with a lot from her. He spent his career living a lie, working against the interests of his superiors for what he'd believed to be the greater good — her greater good. He'd trusted her, and she had done nothing but abuse that relationship.

"Her name is Vivian Ness," Metcalf said. "Ten years ago, I betrayed her team. My team."

"What team?" Kanigher asked. "You told me you were working for —"

"I told you about the FBI, but that was a lie," Metcalf interjected. "I used my time at Quantico to earn the attention of a larger organization, one I was recruited into my first year at the academy."

"Susan, tell me you didn't…"

Metcalf's hand rose to stop him. It had to be said. He needed to hear the words and understand the truth at last. "I spent six years in deep cover with the Trust."

"Dammit, Susan," Kanigher scolded. "Six years?"

"The Madrid mission was my way out," Metcalf said. "It turned out to be the reason I was there in the first place. To find enough evidence to bring them down from the inside. There were no survivors. Or so I thought."

Kanigher paced the room. His hands fell to his hips, his head hung low as he passed back and forth through the small space. "You… You were working for the Trust? When we met, you told me you infiltrated their operations."

"By being recruited," Metcalf said. "Anson Greene brought me in."

It was exactly as she'd intended. She'd learned the tactics, as well as gathered the initial intelligence, from Ben's father. The Trust had been on Kenneth's radar even back then, though the organization had been a little too big for a lone detective in as small a place as Buffalo. His deeds, his dedication to help people, inspired Metcalf to do the same.

Planting herself at Quantico had been the easiest means. Her position as a top recruit put her in Greene's path. It had only been a matter of time before he noticed her. The Trust had been a means to an end. Still, for years, Metcalf had done their dirty work.

Kanigher's problem clearly lay with that slight detail. "You lied to me."

"For your own good," Metcalf replied. She regretted the words immediately. It was proof of her intentions and of her character. There was a reason the team's trust had broken. Kanigher might have been on the fence before, but no longer.

He loomed over her, his warm gaze lost to the cold shadows of the room. "You mean for *your* own good. You played me. After everything I did to secure your freedom, to expunge your record after that mess with Greene. You are some piece of work."

"That I am," Metcalf confirmed without hesitation. "And I am going to pay for it now."

She stood. The door waited, and their time quickly ticked away. Kanigher held her up, a hand before her.

"That's not…" he started, the words unsure and unsteady. Kanigher cursed under his breath. "You can't just go up there."

"I have to. You know I do." She lowered his hand, but held

tight to his calloused fingers for a long moment, before letting them fall away. "This is the right thing, Bobby."

"You want to clear your conscience. There are easier ways to do it, Susan," Kanigher said. "Playing sacrificial lamb gets you nothing but dead."

"You're wrong." Metcalf swiped at the corner of her eye. "It gets you safe. It gives you all a chance to get out of here."

Kanigher offered no other response. His jaw locked shut, and his hands slammed against his sides in frustration. He knew it was the right call for her to head up. It was the only chance the team had to get clear—to save Ben and Morgan from a deep freeze, and restore power to the Bunker.

Metcalf moved for the open door, ready to do her part. Vivian was right to want revenge. All were right to hate and despise Metcalf for all she had done over the years. Human contact, any type of connection, mattered little over the course of her days. The walls she had built because of the trauma of her youth gave her the perfect excuse to act the part of the cold-hearted bitch. She had played the role well.

As she reached the door, Kanigher spoke up. "I'm coming up with her." Metcalf spun on her heels. Kanigher stared up at the camera. "Do you hear me? I'm coming up with her."

"Unacceptable," Vivian responded through the open comm.

"Too bad. I have to." Kanigher turned to Metcalf, sadness in his eyes. "I have to say goodbye."

Silence filled the line. Then a sigh of breath crackled through the speaker. "Very well. Clock's ticking."

Metcalf moved to his side, her voice little more than a whisper. "What are you doing?"

"I don't know yet." Kanigher shrugged his shoulders. He took her by the hand. "I needed a chance to figure this out."

"There's nothing to figure out, Bobby," Metcalf said. "I earned this end. I deserve everything I have coming to me."

CHAPTER EIGHTEEN
Ten Years Ago

Kanigher was out on routine patrol around the perimeter of the military base at Fort Devens. It was another slow night, but then again, after his tours overseas, everything stateside seemed slow to him. He spent his hours imagining a new placement. Kanigher desired a change of pace and thought long and hard about the offer passed to him by the NSA. Government work wasn't ideal for him. He preferred a life in uniform to one in a suit, but he could not deny the benefits of the switch.

What kept him at Fort Devens was his partner, and the man by his side for their nightly patrol: Jacob Grissom. They had served together for years, following each other from station to station. The man was more than a partner or a colleague to Kanigher. After living through the hells they had, there was no one else in the world he would call a brother. They were closer than family, and that made the idea of the NSA a non-starter. Kanigher refused to leave Grissom behind.

In their third hour on patrol around the southeast corner of the complex, their night took a turn neither saw coming. They circled the base on their standard patrol when shots rang out. Two, then three, quick snaps of air resounded through the military base. Both men glanced at each other. No words were necessary, only action.

The shots came from the administrative building near their position. Kanigher and Grissom were, by and far, the closest to the scene, with most of the personnel tucked away in their bunks on the far side of the complex. Even among the other patrols, no one else appeared aware of the situation.

"This way." Grissom swiped his access card for the building. Kanigher stood right behind him. Both prepared for a fight, their sidearms secure in their hands.

"Anyone still logged in?" Kanigher asked. The late hour had sent most people home for the night. Administrative staff typically lived in nearby Ayer. The brass never pulled an all-nighter, not with subordinates more than able to handle the load for them.

Grissom shrugged, scanning the initial corridors for signs of life.

Kanigher checked the log at the welcome desk. A list of names filled the front pages. Arrivals and departures were noted throughout. Only one name remained without a departure time.

"Anson Greene," Kanigher said.

Grissom straightened at the sound of the man's name. Both knew Greene. He was Special Advisor to the base, a title Greene carried everywhere he went, be it government agency, diplomatic embassy, or military installation, where he had a hand in their operations. What that meant, what help he provided, remained a mystery to lowly grunts in uniform.

Grissom had paid a visit or two to the man. He never mentioned their discussions. Kanigher never pushed the issue. To Kanigher, though, Greene wielded too much authority with no oversight from any of the agencies he supposedly served. That made Greene a dangerous figure, and one to stay clear of as much as possible.

Grissom led the way through the office building. They trudged up the steps, then burst through the second floor access door. Greene's office was stationed in the corner. When they arrived, the door was ajar. Grissom paused at the threshold. Kanigher nearly ran into him; Grissom appeared lost on the scene inside.

Kanigher stepped into the room and understood his partner's reaction. "What the hell?"

Greene sat slumped back against the cushion of his chair. Two thin streams of blood ran from the shots to his chest. A third, the kill shot, was positioned in his forehead. No debate sprang up over what had occurred. Their surprise came at the shooter, who stood in the center of the room with her head bowed and the still-smoking gun in her hand.

"Drop the weapon!" Grissom shouted. "Do it now!"

The woman did so without pause. The gun clattered at her side, then settled by her feet. Grissom instantly secured the firearm. He moved to restrain her. His work was efficient, the duty of a soldier in an impossible situation.

Kanigher, however, remained near the door, unsure how to process the scene. More than anything, he was at a loss for the woman's presence. Her cold blue eyes pierced him to his core the moment she looked up at him, her blonde hair tucked in a single tail through the band of her ballcap. She appeared completely out of place on the base, yet her eyes told a very different tale. They spoke of tragedy and pain beyond measure, and they drew Kanigher in with every stray glance shared.

"What have you done?" Grissom looked back to the door, incensed at Kanigher's lack of movement. Grissom cocked his head toward Greene's desk and cleared his throat loudly to draw Kanigher into the room.

"Right," Kanigher muttered. He circled the room, avoiding the eyes of the killer among them. Kanigher checked Greene's vitals. All knew what he would find, yet he still had to try. Greene was dead.

Grissom squeezed the woman's wrists. "I said, what have you done?"

"Killed a traitor," she replied.

Grissom scoffed. "Greene was a patriot! And you—"

"Right pocket." She cut him off. Grissom pulled back, confused at the statement. The woman tucked her head low. "There's a drive in my right pocket. You'll find the evidence on it."

Grissom refused to move for the pocket. He stepped away from the woman and trained his sidearm back on her. Nothing she said resonated with him. Kanigher, however, let curiosity win out. He rounded the desk once more. His fingers dipped cautiously into the pocket of her jeans and retrieved the drive.

"What's on here?"

Grissom shook his head. "I'm calling for backup. We need to inform the brass and see how they want to handle the scene. And her."

Kanigher nodded to his brother-in-arms. He took the drive to Greene's computer.

"Bobby," Grissom called. "Leave it for the brass. This isn't—"

Kanigher continued to place the drive into the computer. He kept his eyes on the woman with the cold blue eyes—so alive, yet so sullen. "What's on here?" he repeated.

"Undercover operatives," she answered. "Their cover identities, and their real ones. Assignments around the globe. Objectives. Everything. He was selling it."

"No way," Grissom snapped. "Greene? He wouldn't. He couldn't. What you're talking about is treason, and Greene—"

"Leave it, Jake," Kanigher said.

The interruption drew Grissom's ire. He raised his weapon to the woman's brow. "No. I won't leave it, Bobby. What she's saying is wrong. It has to be. She's—"

"Not lying." Kanigher spun Greene's laptop to face Grissom. The list was accurate, the intel clear for all to see. A complete list of covert intelligence displayed across the screen. In the wrong hands, it would have meant a lot of spilled blood, and too many bodies on the floor. "It's all here."

"Bobby—"

"Greene wasn't who we thought he was," Kanigher said.

Grissom lowered his weapon. Slow and shuffling steps carried him to the computer. "You don't know where the list came from, Bobby. It could have come from anywhere."

"It's his," the woman said plainly.

Kanigher nodded. "There's more here. Correspondence and records that all tie back to Greene."

Grissom grabbed Kanigher's shoulder. "She killed a man, Bobby. No matter the cause, there are rules we have to follow. She can't just walk away from this."

"I don't intend to." She lifted her bound wrists. "I'm prepared for what comes next."

Grissom wanted to argue more. Worse, he wanted to defend Greene's legacy now that the man had no way to respond to the allegations laid at his corpse. Kanigher knew better. Just as the NSA had approached Kanigher for a position at the agency, he knew Greene had taken an interest in Grissom.

Kanigher had sought to warn his friend, but this served him better. The drive provided hard evidence that backed up the sick feeling he carried whenever the man's name came up in conversation. The drive was irrefutable. With Greene out of the picture,

Grissom was safe from whatever Greene had planned for him. His brother was safe.

As the pair of soldiers escorted the woman from the office, there was only one thing Kanigher could say to show his appreciation to her.

"Thank you."

CHAPTER NINETEEN

Ben continued to wrestle with the door. Morgan thought about it for a moment early on, then resigned herself to the makeshift seat in the center of the freezer. The distance from the vents failed to help her regulate her temperature any better. The cold took root throughout her body and refused to give up its grasp.

She wrapped her arms around her legs to keep what little remained of her body heat. Her fingers were numb, her toes non-existent unless she caught sight of them out of the corner of her eye. She spent every spare ounce of strength on maintaining consciousness.

Time was running out. She could hear it Ben's exasperated breath, and the dimming beat of his hands against the steel. Ben's words continued to resonate with her, and she saw him in a new light.

His doubts went beyond her own. They did not center on Metcalf, and the secrets she had kept from them. For Ben, the DSA as a whole was the culprit for their problems. He questioned everything, and with good reason. From the loss of his former career as a cop to the disappearance of Emily Wright, every event stemmed from the DSA.

He was not the only one with questions. Morgan had heard them from others before. Lincoln had started that line with her after their time in Bellbrook. Then there had been Grissom. Hell, even Stephanie Atwater had chimed in on the debate before her death. Morgan, however, held onto the DSA with everything she had in her.

Ben shuffled away from the door. His breath carried away

from his lips in large drags of mist. He fell against their shared seat, weary and defeated.

"Anything?"

"That thing won't budge," Ben said. He stared at his hands, then shifted to her tucked-in form. Concern for her took over. "You want my shirt?"

"Please don't," Morgan said with a grin. "But thanks."

His arm snuck around behind her and pulled her close. She tried to resist, then nestled against him. Her teeth chattered endlessly. Pressed against Ben's skin, she could feel him shivering. He clearly tried to mute the effects of their prolonged visit to the freezer. The attempt was certainly admirable, but wasted on her.

"The worst part is the lack of food," Ben whined. "I was so looking forward to lunch."

"It's right there." Morgan pointed at their chicken breasts. "Have at it."

"My teeth might shatter just thinking about it."

Morgan laughed. Her lungs burned from the act, and she fell silent. Neither wanted to argue anymore. Neither wanted anything other than to get out of their predicament. Still, Ben's words stuck with her.

"I've questioned the DSA before too," she said. "Just like you."

"Not just like me. I'm—"

"A pain in the ass who has trouble listening?" Morgan remarked sternly. "I'm aware."

"Duly noted," Ben said with a bow of the head. "Continue."

Morgan sighed at his belligerence. "After Grissom, and then after Lincoln, I thought about the DSA and what it meant to me. There had been so much loss, and for what? What the hell had we been doing, and when would it end? Those questions haunted me for so long.

"You know what I figured out?" she continued. "I need the DSA. I need to be right about this place, this team, this mission, or I need to be here to make it right. The work we do, the lives we impact—and what we do makes an impact, Ben, believe that—is too important to throw away."

"I wasn't saying we should—"

Morgan's legs dropped away from her. Her feet slammed to the ground, and she stood to face him. "I offered Holbrook a spot on the team."

"Who?" He stood to join her. "Wait. Holbrook, as in that doctor guy?"

"Yes." Morgan rolled her eyes. "That doctor guy. We sorta got him fired. Okay, I got him fired."

"Yeah, some impact we leave," Ben replied. He ran his hand along the back of his neck.

"Hey," Morgan shot back. "I spent years running, Ben. From my mistakes. From family, friendship, and everything else. This was just a job to me. It was a way to balance the scales for what I screwed up the first time around. That's all I saw for so long. You changed that for me."

"Me?"

"Don't let it swell that mammoth ego." Morgan read his smile well. "But it's true. You made me see this can be more, a chance to really make a difference. How did you always say it? To be a light in the dark."

"I thought you tuned me out," Ben said.

Morgan shifted closer to him. "Don't give up, Ben. Don't throw the DSA away because of Metcalf. Stay. With me."

Ben's gaze fell away. "Morgan, I..."

She shook her head immediately. "Not like that."

"No?"

"Oh, God, no," she answered. She sat back on the seat. "No way."

Ben laughed. "Well, now I feel insulted."

"Don't be an idiot." Morgan slapped the air between them. For the first time in minutes, the cold stopped bothering her. And for the first time in longer than she cared to admit, Morgan felt like the light was brighter on the path ahead—that there was a path ahead for both her and the DSA.

"Susan Metcalf doesn't own the DSA. She doesn't make or break us as a team. We can do this without her. Probably better than she ever did. We can make the DSA work, Ben. But it has to be our choice. Not hers. Not anymore."

CHAPTER TWENTY

Time ticked away. There was no telling how Vivian would react once the ten minutes ran out. Metcalf couldn't take the chance the rest of the team would face her fury, or the repercussions from Metcalf's failure to listen. She started for the door, then paused.

"Susan?" Kanigher continued to stand in the center of the room, shaken and confused. "What is it?"

She beamed at him. "Thank you for standing up for me."

"I don't know if I would call it that." Kanigher's hand ran along the back of his neck. "But we should probably get moving if we—"

Metcalf rushed up to him and kissed him. Surprise greeted her, resistance and shock from Kanigher, but she pushed through it. Her hands nestled along his back, and she continued the kiss. The intensity forced Kanigher back a step, and she twisted them around, their lips locked and their eyes tightly closed.

When she stopped for a breath, he nearly fell over. She held tight to him, his staggered steps positioning him right in front of the camera.

"What was that for?" Kanigher asked, fingers to his lips. "Not that I'm complaining, but—"

Metcalf raised a finger to quiet the question, then spun to face her desk. She ripped open the top drawer and removed a single item. Placing it on her desk, Metcalf turned on the jamming device. The camera on the other side of the room clicked and turned off.

"Wait..." Kanigher noticed the light of the camera fade to

black. "Did you maneuver me to this spot on purpose?"

"Yes."

"So that kiss—"

"Was a diversion," Metcalf said with a furrowed brow. "You knew that, didn't you?"

"How would I know that?" Kanigher read her glare clearly. "Oh, right. We're talking about you here."

"Don't hate the player, hate the game." Metcalf patted his chest with a smile. The flush of his cheeks kept the grin in place as she continued to work around the room.

"What are you doing now?"

Metcalf removed the earpiece from her pocket to show Kanigher. "Hoping my message made it through."

"Message?" Kanigher blinked rapidly. He continued to turn back to the camera, obviously worried the feed would catch their duplicity. "What—"

Metcalf shushed him as she slipped the piece in her ear. "You there, Nixon?"

"I'm here."

"Good," Metcalf said. She pointed to Kanigher's piece. "Comm channel seven."

Kanigher removed the piece, then adjusted the setting. "I'm getting tired of playing 'Follow the Crazy Person.'"

"I thought that was your favorite game," Nixon said through the line.

Metcalf smiled wider. "Tell me where we're at, Nixon."

"Comms are secure as long as we stay on this channel," Nixon said. "Your jammer has overridden the cameras, but it will only last a few minutes."

"Good enough." Metcalf moved for the corridor. Kanigher jumped in front of her to block the door. "Bobby, we need to go."

"No," Kanigher said. "Not without giving me something here."

"You heard Vivian," Metcalf snapped. "If I'm not up there in ten… now, what… six minutes? I have to get moving."

"Yeah, well, you also said this was what you earned for whatever the hell you did to this woman." Kanigher took a sharp breath. "So what's the truth?"

He wasn't wrong. Vivian deserved her revenge. Metcalf,

however, refused to give someone like Vivian leverage over everything she cared about in the world. Her team was in danger, and something had to be done.

"I don't have time to debate you over this," Metcalf said. "Vivian Ness is a dangerous woman. I double-crossed her, for what I still believe to be the right reasons. I thought she was dead. To get you to safety, to get all of you to safety, I'll just have to make damn sure it sticks this time."

"Why?" Kanigher asked. "Why does it have to be you?"

"She's expecting me," Metcalf replied, confused. "She—"

"I know, I know," Kanigher said. "I have an idea about that, though."

"Why does that worry me?"

"Because it should." He backpedaled into the hallway. Metcalf moved to follow. "I'd certainly feel much more confident about it if we had a secondary exit to exploit." He continued toward the main door, now unlocked for their use of the elevator. Metcalf remained in front of her quarters, unmoved. "Susan?"

"We do."

"We do, what?"

"There's another way out of the Bunker," Metcalf said.

Kanigher's eyes widened. "There's... You know what? I'm not going to bother arguing about another secret right now."

"There is the time constraint," Metcalf replied with a smirk.

Kanigher shook his head. "Lucky you."

They quickened down the corridor. They passed the bathrooms, skirted by the mainframe womb and a curious Nixon, and around the training facility. The journey ended at the end of the second turn. Their race took them around the half-circle loop that made up the complex. A sealed wall of bricks barred them from continuing.

"Here?"

Metcalf reached for a false brick in the upper corner of the wall. She pushed it in until the mechanism clicked and a door opened. "Here."

A tunnel led into the darkness. Kanigher stood before the opening, hands to his hips. "Unbelievable."

Metcalf patted his back. "Is your plan going to distract her long enough?"

"It will get you in play. But after that?"

She nodded. There was always going to be risk. It was part of the job, the part she typically left to her team. This time, the danger fell to her, and Metcalf felt more than ready to take it on. This was, after all, her mess to clean up.

"Nixon? Adler?" she called through the comm.

"We're here," Nixon said.

"Vivian is using an external control console to overwrite the Bunker's protocols," Metcalf said. "You need to reboot the system to bring it back under our control."

"There's an external control center?" Nixon asked.

"We can talk about it later, Nixon." Metcalf cut off the man's curiosity. They were on the clock. "Can you do it, Alison?"

"I have to," the overwhelmed tech muttered through the line.

"Yes, you do." Metcalf tapped the comm, ending the call. "Bobby?"

He nodded. "We're down to five minutes. I better hurry."

She grabbed his hand and squeezed. "Thank you for trusting me on this."

"I don't," Kanigher said. "So earn it, Susan. Make it right. For everyone."

CHAPTER TWENTY-ONE

The feeds went blank. Vivian slammed her hands against the control panel. This was exactly what she had tried to avoid. There was no need for unnecessary violence and bloodshed. This was about Metcalf, and only her.

Vivian sat back down. Prompts arose on the screen; each required the access codes she had hacked days earlier. She inputted the series, careful not to make a mistake. When complete, the prompt faded and a status bar appeared. Vivian watched it crawl across the screen.

Had she done something wrong? Or had Metcalf gone against her word in a desperate attempt to escape her fate?

The cameras clicked back on. Nixon remained outside the mainframe womb. The freezer door was still shut and locked, the two field agents trapped inside. Kanigher escorted Metcalf out of the Bunker's main entrance and down the corridor to the elevator.

Vivian breathed a sigh of relief. Nothing would deter her revenge. She slid back from the console, content the players were moving toward their respective positions. Leaving the control room behind, she grabbed the rifle resting along the wall. Once Metcalf reached the surface, it would be over.

Years of patience and preparation had built to this moment. Years of pain and judgment, of lives lost, brought her to the cusp of a new dawn.

They didn't listen.

Six hours in conference with the heads of the Central Intelligence Agency, and Vivian stepped out of the room with only one conclusion: the word intelligence held no meaning for the men inside. For all their sympathy, for all their vain attempts to consider her circumstances with the so-called utmost care, they spent more time talking down to her like a child than recalling her dedicated career in the organization.

Vivian held her tongue through it all. She sat through the never-ending reports drawn up, the evaluations she had undertaken to even make it in the room, as well as the endless statements that opened and closed each board member's time on the floor.

None of them actually said anything of merit. They touted fancy narratives of little substance. Every word attempted to soften the blow, when in truth, all they did was diminish her.

"You're firing me?" Vivian asked at the end of it all. Throughout the proceedings, no one said anything differently. They offered no placement, no position in the field or even in an office.

"No, not at all," the man at the head of the table replied. "That's not what this is."

Vivian shook her head. She held up the final report offered by the board. "It says DISCHARGED at the top."

"Completely different from firing," another man said. So many men in the room, yet none had the balls to look in her direction. They passed smiles back and forth to each other rather than face her pain directly. "A discharge means you'll be covered for life, Agent Ness. Full benefits for your exceptional service to your country."

Vivian slammed the paper on the desk. "I don't want this. You can keep your benefits. I just want my job back. I want my life back."

"I'm afraid that won't be possible," the man at the head said. "Your injuries, your handicap…"

"There really is no simple way to say this, Agent Ness," the other continued. "We are proud of the work you've done for us in the past, but going forward? Well, I'm afraid that time is over."

"You're taking away my chance at answers," Vivian said through clenched jaw. "What happened to me was wrong."

"And we have investigated the matter fully."

"We continue to search for the members of the Order of the Fallen," another chimed in. "There will be a full accounting. Have no doubt about that."

"It's more than some investigation," Vivian snapped. "More than a simple accounting. To me, it's about getting my life back. This job is all I have left. You can't do this to me."

"Unfortunately, we have to." The man at the head of the table shut his report and his hand rested on the cover. "This matter is closed. I'm sorry."

"So am I," Vivian muttered, before stomping from the room. It was a waste of time, like so much had been since her return. She had never bothered to reconnect with anyone from her past. What little remained of her family and friends had all moved on with their lives, while she obsessed over the moment of her death.

Part of her yearned to return to Spain, and her time as Nina. There had been peace in her life thanks to the ignorance of her broken memory. The notion was impossible, though, not without knowing the truth about what happened to her.

She left the conference room, defeated. There was nowhere else for her to turn, no one to reach out to for help. She had read plenty of public records; casefiles had shown her to be a competent and well-respected agent, but little else. She was still incomplete, yet revenge dug its way into her heart and refused to abate.

Revenge offered closure, but without a clear target Vivian continued to spiral in a never-ending descent. As she passed the elevators for the stairs, she stopped at the sight of a man waiting for her.

"You."

Hollis wore a pale suit jacket over khakis. He leaned against the wall, but pushed away from it at her approach. She hadn't seen him since that day in Spain, when he told her the truth about the person she had been and could be again.

He read the aggravation in her face clearly. "They couldn't be bothered, could they?"

"I don't need your pity on top of everything else." Vivian pushed through him.

"Not offering any." Hollis caught her by the wrist. "I'm only looking to help."

"Like you did before?" Vivian pulled free from the man's grip. "I was happy in Spain. Why couldn't you just let me be happy?"

"That was a lie, Vivian," he said. "This is who you are. If they can't see that, then it's their loss."

"If they can't see it, maybe they're right to let me go."

"You don't believe that."

"I don't believe anything at the moment." Vivian reached for the stairwell door. "Now if you'll excuse me?"

"I know what you need," Hollis called after her. Her hand slipped from the knob. "What keeps you up at night. It isn't what happened in Madrid. Anyone can tell you that. The doctor's already told you that much."

Vivian's hand instinctively moved for her dead eye.

"A bullet took your eye and stole your life." Hollis slipped in close to her. His fingers wrapped around her own and lowered her hand from her eye. "What if I told you the name of the woman who fired that bullet? What if I told you how you can get your revenge, how you can finally get your life back? Would that help?"

Susan Metcalf.

It was funny how something as simple as a name could jumpstart a person's core. The second Hollis told her about Metcalf, she felt as if she had been struck by lightning. Everything crystallized.

With Hollis' resources, Vivian had learned all there was to know about Metcalf. She'd followed all the news about the woman's time with the DSA. Then Vivian had gone back further—right to the farmhouse of her birth.

Vivian had been under orders to bring her findings to Hollis. She had been expected to keep him apprised of her research. Instead, Vivian had told no one.

This was for her—for her future. Vivian had to be the one to finish this mission on her own.

Four minutes remained on the counter. Vivian secured the rifle in her grasp and moved for the door. For the first time in a long time, she allowed herself a smile.

"No more pain. No more nightmares. Finally, this ends."

CHAPTER TWENTY-TWO

Metcalf stepped through the emergency hatch. She quickly closed the door to the Bunker behind her, dropping the entire hall into deep shadows. In the distance was a flicker of light.

The corridor held no traditional flooring. Planks supported the tunnel cut through the heart of the hillside in the back of the expansive property. The hatch was never meant to be used in this manner, nor at all really.

Sheer safety had been the reason for its inclusion in the original plans. Having only one egress never made sense to Metcalf. Somehow, in her warped need for control, hiding multiple exit points from everyone made complete and total sense by comparison. She understood the truth behind her decision to hold another secret from the team. It was why she'd destroyed the original blueprints immediately upon construction. Secrets were a means of control to Metcalf. They made her irreplaceable.

The planks rattled beneath her. Like the rungs of a ladder, they dug into her knees as she crawled deeper through the tightening corridor. The hatch led to an exhaust port out the back of the hillside. Once out in the open, it would take what precious few minutes remained to circle back to the front where the target would no doubt be lying in wait.

As she reached the incline at the crook in the planking, her watch rang out. Another minute had slipped away from her, and left her with only three. At the sound of the slight ding, Kanigher's voice filled her ear through the comm link.

"This is stupid," he uttered.

His words brought a smile to her face. She could hear the thrum of the elevator rising to the surface. It forced her to move faster, though she could not possibly match the pace because of the tight quarters surrounding her.

"This was your idea," she replied.

"Why do you think I said it?"

His lack of confidence startled her. Kanigher never held so many doubts before. He never had a reason to before. Now, there was nothing but mistrust and anxiety. Metcalf let him down repeatedly; the latest news about her ties to the Trust cemented the notion that the secrets would never end with her.

She refused to let him down again—or anyone else from the team. Ben and Morgan counted on them for rescue. Their survival mattered to Metcalf, no matter what either of them thought of her. The DSA was more than a mission to her; the people she'd brought with her on the journey remained her true heart and soul.

The incline crested, then twisted once more. At the end of the path ahead, a stream of light shimmered through the grating. Metcalf pushed harder, her knees scraping along the metal planks.

"It's too open out there," Kanigher said. The elevator came to a grinding halt. The doors opened with a groan. "We'll be sitting ducks."

"Not you," Metcalf reminded him. "Me."

"Susan, I'm sorry about—"

"Let's get this over with, Bobby," she interrupted. She didn't deserve his apology. She certainly had done little to deserve his friendship for so long. Metcalf hoped to change that somehow. She needed the chance to make that change.

"Good luck."

The comm link went silent. Metcalf's time ran out. She reached for the grating. Hands dug in and pushed with all her might. Weeds had snaked around the outskirts. Layers of dirt and untrimmed sod threatened to lock her in place.

"Don't you even think about it," Metcalf grumbled. She cried out, throwing all her frustrations into the act. The lock turned in her hand and pushed out. Broken and unsettled earth fell away, and the hatch opened to the mid-afternoon sky.

Metcalf climbed free. She sought to catch her breath. Her heart raced in her chest and her body burned in the heat of the sun. All she wanted was a moment of rest. Her watch, however, made it clear the chance for rest had long since passed. Her sidearm slid loose from its holster and Metcalf brought it before her. She ran for the other side of the hill.

"It's time to end this."

CHAPTER TWENTY-THREE

The shot rang out. The body fell from the impact into the lawn separating the farmhouse and the Bunker.

"No!" Kanigher cried. "Susan!"

He tapped his comm twice, then bolted from the elevator. He carried no weapon, no deterrent to save him from the shooter's wrath. Still, Kanigher raced ahead. From across the field, he noticed Vivian. Positioned outside the home in a row of bushes, her rifle poked through the branches for a clear shot.

He skidded to a halt beside his fallen colleague. Cradling her body in his arms, Kanigher turned his back to the shooter. With the body of Vivian's victim obscured from view, Kanigher ran his hand through her hair. Beneath the blonde wig, the metallic sheen of one of Nixon's robotic training dummies clicked and whirred.

"Turn it off," Kanigher whispered under his breath. "Nixon, I need you to—"

"It's done," Nixon replied.

The bot fell slack against Kanigher's arms. It was the only option he could think of in the time allotted. Vivian had been expecting Metcalf, and he couldn't let her make such a sacrifice. There had, of course, been the option of body armor, but the risk of a high caliber bullet or a well-placed shot to the head instead of the chest took that out of the running.

No, Kanigher needed to buy Metcalf time. This move brought Vivian out into the open. It also allowed Kanigher to revel in his finest acting moment.

"Why, Susan, why?" he said, loud enough for Vivian to hear. Behind him, the rustle of branches gave way to approaching steps.

"Really, Robert?" Nixon chirped in his ear. "Laying it on a bit thick, aren't you?"

"I'm hoping it pisses her off enough to make a mistake." Kanigher fixed the wig in place to bury the metal shell beneath the thick strands. The rest of the dummy was dressed head to toe to keep the frame hidden.

"Well, I think the robot is the better actor," Nixon commented.

"Let's hope all the time you spent building the damn thing wasn't for nothing." Kanigher lowered the body back to the ground. He forced out sorrowful sobs at the passing of his dear friend.

"Back off!" Vivian shouted from behind him. Kanigher raised his hands and struggled to his feet. He was clearly too slow in the effort as a shot echoed through the air. "The deal was simple. She's mine!"

Kanigher turned to face Vivian. He kept his hands raised. "You have what you want already."

"Not yet, I don't," Vivian sneered. Kanigher noted the dead right eye. A scar ran through it. The woman remained undeterred from the injury, weapon held tight in her left hand and aimed directly at Kanigher. "Now back the hell away."

"Okay, just—"

He pushed things too far. Her impatience won out, and Vivian opened fire.

"Dammit." Kanigher leaped to the side, then rolled with the impact on the earth. Jumping to his feet, Kanigher ran for the still open elevator. Shots followed him the entire way. They skidded off the ground to his right and pinged along the metal of the hillside door frame.

"Kanigher?" Adler's voice called out through the comm. "Kanigher!"

He was cut off from the door controls, pinned on the opposite side of the elevator. When he shifted to the open door, a shot caused him to duck once more. "I'm okay. Just need some cover."

"I thought she only wanted Metcalf?"

"Did you not hear his terrible acting?" Nixon asked. "I'm surprised he's not dead already."

"Nixon!" Adler yelled.

Kanigher tried for the controls once more. A stray bullet ricocheted off the back wall and cut across his arm. Kanigher winced in pain and tucked the wound tight to his chest. He curled deeper into the corner of the elevator car for cover.

"Shit." He held the cut to staunch the bleeding. The stream flowed under his grasp, and pain pulsed up his arm.

"What is it?"

"She has me pinned," Kanigher said. "She's almost to Metcalf's body. If I can't get the doors closed in time, she's going to be one very pissed off woman with only one potential target on hand."

"Nixon?" Adler said.

"Are you talking to me again?"

Adler groaned through the line. "We don't have time for this."

"I'd say there's at least twenty to thirty seconds…"

"Nixon!"

Kanigher peered around the corner. Vivian kept her sidearm poised and ready to fire. She was getting closer to the fake Metcalf's body. If she only focused on the fallen, there was every chance she'd notice the swap pulled against her.

"I'm trying, Robert." The sound of tapping keys filled the line. "We're still limited with what we can—"

"Forget it," Kanigher replied. "I've got it."

"Kanigher, you—"

He turned off the comm. Standing, Kanigher pushed through the pain in his arm and the threat outside. He bolted for the far side of the car and the waiting controls.

Vivian tracked his movements and opened fire. The shots hit behind him as Kanigher dove for the operating panel. His finger depressed the door control, and the elevator shook with motion.

Kanigher crashed to the ground and slid to a halt against the wall of the car. The thud of the doors closing silenced Vivian's fury and dropped Kanigher into darkness.

He struggled to sit upright, his back against the wall. Tapping the comm line open once more, the arguing of his colleagues greeted him; both were concerned for his safety.

Kanigher ended their chatter. "Guys, I'm all right."

"You are?" Nixon asked.

"Thank God," Adler said.

"I'm heading down now." He had done all he could for Metcalf. He hoped it had been enough. "Looks like it's all on you now, Adler."

CHAPTER TWENTY-FOUR

The wire slipped from Adler's hand. It fell to her side, lost in a bevy of similar connections. Cursing her luck, Adler focused on the thin light from atop her glasses to find the needle in the stack of needles. She sought the latest in a series of attachments in her effort to reboot the Bunker's massive mainframe.

The process was slow-going, much too slow for the situation occurring around them. The constant pressure placed upon her by Kanigher and Metcalf was not helping matters, either. Everything rested on her shoulders now. All of their lives were at stake, especially Ben's and Morgan's who remained trapped in the freezer.

"I can't do this." Adler shook the wires for the loose one in the bunch. The proper connector refused to show itself in her hunt. Adler squeezed the pack, then pushed them all away in frustration. "I just can't do this!"

Adler sunk to the ground of the womb. She pulled the glasses from her eyes and set them on her head. Closing her eyes, Adler took a second to catch her breath. She tried to push through the heat of the mainframe and the constant humming in her ears.

None of this was meant to be put on her. She was a simple tactician. When called in, Adler did the job, then went home. It was easy, and it was fun. Situations like this were too much for her.

Zac would have known what to do. The mainframe, computers in general, had always been his strength. He had been great at pretty much everything. In a single day, he managed everything and everyone within the DSA. He'd known exactly who had worked on what case, who had pulled which report from the server, and how many freaking cups of coffee they had had in the process.

Adler did not know how he had done it all. She never trained for the high-pressure situations. She wanted nothing more in life than to serve a higher purpose and make her parents proud.

"Alison?" Nixon called through the comm.

Adler opened her eyes. She fumbled with the glasses tangled in her hair, then set them back on the bridge of her nose. "I can't do this, Nixon."

"You can."

"Don't talk to me like that," Adler shot back. "Don't pretend a positive attitude and a healthy outlook are going to win the day here. I can't see. I don't know this system like you. Like Zac would. I'm hungry, I'm sweating, and I can't save anyone."

"Too bad."

Adler's eyes widened. "What?"

"You heard me," Nixon said. "Too bad. It's all on you."

"You're not really helping."

"I tried to help," Nixon said. "You yelled at me."

"I didn't—"

"It's all right. I'm used to it." Nixon took a breath. The confidence in his voice startled her. It shook her back to her feet. "Usually it means I've touched a nerve, or cracked a code I wasn't meant to crack. I'm assuming it's the pressure of never measuring up to the sainted Zachary Modine you people keep mentioning in passing."

"He wasn't sainted. It's that he—"

"Was an idiot."

"Excuse me?"

"I met the man twice before," Nixon said. "Both times at big tech conferences. I wasn't there for the lectures. More of a way to gain a leg up on the competition."

"You stole their specs," Adler commented.

"Hey, if they didn't want to protect their precious investment with a decent firewall, they can't really blame me, can they?"

"Pretty sure they can."

Nixon grumbled under his breath. "Anyway, I bump into the great Mr. Modine, and he can't even be bothered. He's there to recruit for a secret think-tank, and looking for someone in particular. He's going on and on about her, like she was the second coming. When he pointed her out, I couldn't believe it. You ever hear of Francine Szabo?"

"Maybe? Nixon, I—"

"She built a multi-channel datanet for storing massive amounts of system information," Nixon said. "Terrific with tech, terrible with people."

"Sounds familiar."

"It was exactly what the DSA needed at the time to build their queue," Nixon continued. "That was how Zac saw the world. Same as Metcalf. There was the DSA, and nothing else. Nothing and no one stood in his way."

"I still don't get your point," Adler asked.

"My point is that I stopped Zac and told him he was wrong," Nixon said. "I told him he was looking in the wrong place completely, and I pointed to someone else at the conference, someone who was working through the circles of people and finding out about every little thing being done there. Who they were, why they wanted to be the next best thing in tech, and where things were heading."

"Nixon..." Adler said. "Are you talking about the Developer Conference?"

"I am."

"In Austin?"

"Indeed."

"I was at that show," Adler whispered.

Nixon chuckled. "Who the hell do you think I've been talking about?"

"I don't..."

"Zac was looking at tech," Nixon said. "You were looking at people. He's the idiot who picked the wrong side in the end. You're the genius who is going to save our asses."

"That doesn't make this any easier." Adler moved within the tunnel for the wires once more. "I don't know if I can—"

"Dear God, woman!" Nixon bellowed in her ear. "How can you throw away that incredibly nostalgic-laden story I just threw at you? That was a Braveheart-level performance on my part!"

"You're no Mel Gibson."

"Thank heaven for that small favor." Nixon took a deep breath. His voice softened. "The truth is, no matter what you think of yourself, no matter who you believe to be better suited for the task ahead, it's yours and yours alone in there. If you don't do this, Ben and Morgan freeze to death. If you can't swallow your doubts, and bury your fear of failure, Robert and Susan will die at the hands of this lunatic woman."

Adler closed her eyes. She dipped her hands into the wires. Carefully, she pried apart the connections knotted together that blocked most of the tunnel until she found the loose one she had lost. She allowed a brief smirk, then slipped the adapter into the waiting slot.

"Your motivational speeches need work," Adler said. "But thank you, Nixon."

"Happy to help."

Adler shifted deeper into the web. "I've got this. I just need a little more time."

CHAPTER TWENTY-FIVE

Vivian's heart raced. It was finally over. She released the spent clip of her sidearm, a Sig Sauer P320. It crashed to the flattened earth near her feet. Reaching along her belt, Vivian freed a fresh clip and inserted it into the base of the weapon.

The air seemed cleaner to her, the scent of budding flowers and growing grass more vibrant. Everything brightened in the aftermath. No one stood between her and her victim. The duplicitous Agent Kanigher was well on his way back down to the Bunker. He would keep for a little longer. At the moment, Vivian held no more room in her heart for the rage and anger that had consumed her for so long. There was only a rebirth, thanks to the death of Susan Metcalf.

"I can't believe it's over," she said. Her slow walk carried her closer to the body. The woman did not move; the shot had been precise to the center of her chest. There would be no walking away from that. "So much preparation, so much anticipation. If only I could watch you die over and over again."

Vivian closed her eyes. The sound of the bullet escaping the barrel of the rifle filled her ears. She smelled the powder in the air, and the recoil continued to sting her shoulder. The sensation sent a wave of ecstasy through her body when the shot hit her target, and Metcalf fell to the ground.

"Mmmm," she moaned with pleasure, then opened her eyes. "I'll take my revenge, though, no matter how quickly it was attained."

She crouched next to the body, careful to keep Metcalf in full view of her one good eye. Her gun remained trained on her as a precaution, though she noticed Metcalf's chest failed to rise and fall from even the shallowest breath.

"Knowing you died at my hand will always put a smile on my face," Vivian said. "As will the fact that none of your so-called team will leave that bunker alive."

Things were always going to end that way. She could not take the chance on any retribution. Closing the loop here and now gave her the opportunity to finish the mission and reclaim her life again. That was all Vivian wanted — the sum total of her being. What that life entailed remained a mystery, but one she looked forward to solving.

The past would be a memory Vivian hoped to forget completely. From Metcalf herself, and the role she'd played in her initial demise, to Hollis for pulling her back and killing her a second time, all the way through the collapse of the DSA — locked and buried forever in their hidden headquarters.

"Thank you for setting me free," Vivian said. She leaned close to the body. Her hand pulled away the blonde strands over Metcalf's face. Vivian needed to see the terror in her foe's eyes when she met her end, to know Metcalf felt the same fear that had surrounded Vivian's life ever since their first unfortunate meeting.

"Wait," Vivian said. "What's this?"

With the hair pulled back, no fear sat in the woman's eyes. There was not the terror Vivian imagined in her mind, only the metallic sheen of a construct — not flesh and bone at all.

Vivian ripped the wig from the dummy. She tore at the clothing hiding the metal shell. A scream of anger erupted from her core, rage at the ploy and how easily she had fallen for it in her zeal.

"No!" she bellowed. Vivian pounded against the chest of the de-powered decoy. "No, no, no, no!"

Her chest heaved. All contentment with the day slipped away from her. The fragrant smell of the air no longer penetrated her nostrils, and the light of the sun dimmed behind a stray cloud rolling over the field.

"It can't be," Vivian muttered. She clambered back to her feet, scrambling away from the fallen diversion. "I heard your voice. I watched you get on that damn elevator."

Vivian stomped over to the hillside. She raised the Sig Sauer to the control panel outside the wide frame. "I watched you die!"

Vivian's cry fell to the background as she opened fire at the panel. The display shattered from the onset, the circuits beneath pummeled by the subsequent bullets ripping into the guts of the system.

There would be no escaping the Bunker now… for any of them.

Vivian staggered back. Her finger still pulled the trigger of her empty weapon. "You can't do this to me. I killed you!"

"You did a piss-poor job of it, then."

Standing over the metallic corpse was the woman Vivian had been chasing. It was the woman who haunted her nightmares and kept her from her dreams.

"You."

Metcalf nodded. She raised her hand and waved her opponent closer. "You want your revenge? Come and get it."

CHAPTER TWENTY-SIX

"That one," Nixon said through the comm. "Over to the right. Yes."

Adler jammed the wire into place, and a panel opened along the wall. Microchips ran in four long rows that stretched over a yard in length.

She swiped at the sweat on her brow, then ran her hands along her pants to accomplish the same goal. It did little to aid her discomfort in the narrow corridor behind the mainframe.

"I'm in. Are you seeing this?"

"Barely," Nixon said. "There must be some interference from being so close to the terminals. Audio is coming in clear, but the glasses aren't giving me a decent picture to help."

"Of course not." Adler removed the lenses. Sweat dripped across the screens. Fog dotted the corners from the oppressive heat surrounding her.

"Adler?" Kanigher called. The sound of the elevator opening rang in the background. His pounding feet against the floor quickly replaced it. "We're out of time."

"Do you think I don't already know that?" she yelled through the comm. A chip fell between her fingers. It landed on her other palm, and she clutched it tight. A sigh of relief escaped, yet was subsumed by trepidation as she reversed the chip's position on the board. It locked into place with a loud click.

"Listen," Kanigher said through heavy breaths. "I need Ben and Morgan in the field. I can't—"

"Alison is well aware, Robert," Nixon interrupted. "She is working as fast as she can. There's no need for more pressure."

"Thank you, Nixon." She switched another chip out, this time with the row beneath. Nothing was labeled clearly. Numbers represented the different circuits which controlled each section of the Bunker. To reboot the system, Adler knew every single section required the switch.

"Still, if you could—"

Adler huffed. "And the thank you has been rescinded."

"Sorry," Nixon said. "Are the chips—"

"They are almost in place." She lifted the last one from its cradle and swapped the chip out with one from the bottom row. "All set."

"I'm still in the dark here," Kanigher said.

"We're not finished yet," Nixon replied. Adler could practically hear the tech's eyes roll during the response.

"Dammit," Kanigher groaned. "Listen, I'm heading for the tunnel now. Nixon, when the system is set, I need you to get the others topside as soon as possible. Especially Morgan, just in case Metcalf is—"

"We're working here, Kanigher!" Adler shouted. Her frustration filled the line in a harrowing scream. She tried to catch her breath. She tried to picture the next step, one Nixon had gone over with her several times. Everything was delicate, everything was painstaking, and all rested in her hands. Her self-doubts no longer held sway over her. Adler needed to finish the job, for all their sakes.

"Got it," Kanigher said. "She's all yours, Nixon."

"You're doing fine, Alison," Nixon said in a soft tone. No more lectures followed—no more pushing and prodding for her to do more and be more. All were well aware of what was at stake.

She reconnected the wiring surrounding the chips. The panel pulled back into place. Nothing happened: no burst of cool air from the ventilation systems kicking back on, no lights from the control panels, not even the faint hum of the server fans.

"Oh, no." Adler fell back to a sitting position. "It didn't work."

"You're not done yet," Nixon said.

"I'm not?" Adler asked. How could she not be done? She followed his instructions to the letter, been locked inside the damn mainframe for what felt like hours because of her ridiculous need to track a damn signal that might not actually matter to anyone or anything in the world. For all she had known, the signal had been nothing more than a fluke of nature, the great whale to her Ahab-like search. "Nixon?"

"The main reset is back the way you came. If the chips are in the correct order —"

"They are," she said through clenched teeth.

"I'm sure they are," Nixon said. "All you need to do is throw the reset switch, wait thirty seconds, then pop it back into place."

"Yeah." Adler shook her head. "That's all. Lucky me."

Adler crawled through the tunnels within the mainframe. She pulled her tired body under the massive cables that crisscrossed the system in a giant web. All her fiddling might not have brought light to the place, or a cool breeze to counter the heat of the mainframe, but what it had done was illuminate the reset switch. It sat on the wall opposite her position. A dim, red glow emanated from the handle.

"I see it."

"You've got this, Alison," Nixon said. "Just reach out…"

"If you say touch someone, I'm going to belt you in the face."

"No one appreciates the classics anymore."

"Oh, I think I'm going to appreciate a lot more the second this is over," Adler said. "Here goes."

Her hand cradled the switch. With all her strength, Adler forced it down until a loud click echoed in the chamber. A mental countdown started behind her eyes. The ticking clock rang loudly in her mind, while silence surrounded her. Even Nixon held his breath, a pleasant change of pace from the endless wheezing picked up by her earpiece.

"Twenty-eight, twenty-nine… thirty," Adler counted. Her hand remained on the switch. They were screwed if this didn't work. "Fingers crossed."

Fans kicked into gear all around her. Cool air rushed through the ventilation chambers that marked every corridor in the complex. From beyond the mainframe womb, Adler saw light return to the Bunker.

"You did it!" Nixon exclaimed, pure joy in the man's voice. "You actually did… I mean… way to go, Alison."

Adler collapsed to her knees. A smile filled her face. "I did it."

CHAPTER TWENTY-SEVEN

Vivian looked just like Metcalf remembered. Their time in Madrid — brief as it might have been for her — had been etched in her mind for almost a decade. So important were the events of that day, Metcalf kept her plane ticket in the small metal box of mementos locked in her quarters.

All of her mistakes ended up in her box. Few ever made their way out, yet here was Vivian standing before her, a prime example that the past always returned... one way or another.

Her actions that day trailed her long after Metcalf had left the Temple of Debod. The dead had not been planned, her betrayal more of a spur-of-the-moment deal than a carefully outlined mission. She had spent years searching for a way to bring down Greene. Metcalf had done everything possible to find something to shatter the Trust within the confines of the law. That day in Madrid she'd learned the truth: the law held no sway over some people. A different kind of justice waited for them, and Metcalf's actions in the temple had set her on a path to enact them against both Greene and the Trust.

Vivian, however, clearly hadn't come to hear any explanation for what had happened so long ago. She had come for only one thing, something Metcalf understood deeply, having done the same to Greene: Vivian Ness wanted her revenge.

"This doesn't have to end with any bloodshed, Vivian," Metcalf said. She stood behind the fallen training dummy, her supposed decoy. A thin glance at the metallic shell, Metcalf wondered how the hell Kanigher thought his plan would work. She was surprised the ruse lasted as long as it had. She put it aside and caught the fury in her opponent's eyes. "What happened to you—"

"What happened to me?" Vivian shouted. "You tried to kill me! You did kill me in every way that matters. By the time I found my way home, I had nothing left. No career, no friends, and no loved ones. They all moved on. All I have left is you and my revenge."

"I'm sorry," Metcalf said. "But I made the right call."

"You betrayed us!" Vivian yelled. She stalked closer, the gun tight in her hand. She raised it to meet Metcalf's chest. "You think you did the right thing? I was an agent of the CIA!"

Metcalf's brow furrowed. "Is that… Is that what you remember?"

"That's the truth!"

"According to whom?" Metcalf lowered her weapon and inched closer to the woman. "You don't remember what happened that day, do you? Someone told you a story, Vivian, and they left out the juicy bits for their benefit."

"Liar."

"Who was it? Couldn't have been Greene," Metcalf pressed. Vivian's grip slackened on the gun, her fingers shaking. "Hollis?"

Recognition flashed in Vivian's eye.

Metcalf nodded. "David Hollis. The bastard."

"He told me everything," Vivian said. "You infiltrated my CIA team. You murdered us for classified intel."

"I saved that intel from ending up in the hands of a terrorist group," Metcalf snapped. "Terrorists you were making a deal with."

Vivian shook her head. "I was a good agent. I served my country!"

"You served yourself!" Metcalf shouted. "Worse, you served people like Greene and Hollis, without a single thought about what the hell they were working on, or who they were working with. They used you, and Hollis is still using you. Vivian, you weren't some CIA agent—not really, anyway. You worked for a group hidden within law enforcement and the military. You worked for a group called the Trust."

"No," Vivian muttered, her left eye heavy with tears. "I was loyal to my country. I would have done anything to keep people safe."

"Then why were you selling out your people so easily?" Metcalf asked. "You would have exposed every covert agent in the world. You would have betrayed your country for the Trust, Vivian."

"Never!" Vivian crumbled from the accusation. She retreated into herself and her faulty memory for comfort. She shook her head vigorously. There was no more reasoning with her. She held onto the only truth she cared to know. "You're the traitor! You killed my team!"

"I'm sorry for what happened, Vivian," Metcalf said. "I truly am. But you're on the wrong side of this one. Please don't fight me. Surrender, and I will see to it we make things right. For you. And against the Trust for manipulating you."

"No." Vivian pulled the trigger of her Sig Sauer. The clip had long since been emptied in her rage. Vivian tossed the gun aside and screamed. She rushed at Metcalf. Only the need for blood remained, and nothing would stand in her way.

"Vivian—"

The woman slammed into Metcalf. Both hit the ground and rolled from the impact. Metcalf shoved her attacker aside and clambered to her feet. She leveled her sidearm at Vivian.

"Don't make me kill you."

Metcalf took aim. The woman's fury made it impossible to reason with her, to find a common ground from which to calm down. All Vivian saw in Metcalf was the villain of her story.

All Metcalf saw was another victim left to rot in the trash heap that was her past. With every stolen glance of the woman, Metcalf's resolve faltered. Slowly, her weapon lowered, until she dropped it to the soft grass. She kicked it away and shook her head.

"I won't do it," Metcalf said. "I won't kill you."

"Because you can't. You tried and failed before," Vivian replied. Her fists clenched before her. Saliva dripped from her lips with anticipation. She cocked back her left arm, then shot forward for Metcalf. "I won't."

CHAPTER TWENTY-EIGHT

Ben took Morgan's words to heart. Her need for the DSA to be right made sense—their shared struggle to help others paramount to moving forward. Still, Ben hesitated to act. Metcalf's betrayal remained too raw to react without understanding the consequences of removing her from the team.

Too many questions trailed his spinning thoughts. Metcalf's relationship with Ben's father had weighed on his mind. He had held back asking for more information, fought the urge to listen to war stories about his old man, yet clung to the hope that eventually they would come to light. That time, however, had passed with her connection to the Witness exposed to the rest of the team. Now he worried Metcalf's history would always remain hidden, even from him. The thought saddened him and brought more doubts to the surface.

Of all the questions rattling around in his nearly frozen brain, there was one Ben answered with absolute confidence. He held no regret, no trepidation, about his time with Morgan, and knew the only way forward was if the two of them remained together. No one in the world—even Emily Wright, if Ben was being honest with himself—had come to mean more to him than Morgan Dunleavy. Through everything, she had stood by his side. If Morgan needed the DSA, who was he to stand in her way?

"You're right, Morgan," Ben said. The pair continued to press tight together. The cold clung to them like a waxy coating along their skin. "We have to stand together. Now more than ever. This last year has been, well, a nightmare, to be honest. But the one bright spot has been you, and I—"

A snap stole his words, and their shared attention. They

turned to the freezer door — the source of the sound — to see the door ajar. Light shone through from the kitchen.

"Did that —" Morgan struggled to ask the question.

Ben didn't need to hear it, anyway. He fought to stand, his knees barely able to bend. "The door's open."

He held out his hand. Morgan took it and stood by his side. The pair staggered forward across the expanse of the freezer. They pushed through the cold mist that washed over them. They leaned into the walk, careful not to fall for fear they would never get back up again.

Ben let Morgan go as they reached the door. He blocked her escape, a lone finger raised. "Hang back a second. Just in case."

Morgan shook her head. Her entire body shivered from the cold. "The hell with that."

Grabbing the handle, Morgan pushed the door open. It slammed against the far wall. Heat greeted them and sent waves of pleasure through their bodies as they stepped out of their cage.

"Dear God, that feels good," Morgan said.

"I forgot to grab the chicken." Ben pointed back inside. "Should I —"

"Don't be an idiot."

"Can I be hungry?"

Morgan glared at him.

"Are you two done?" a voice called from the other side of the counter.

"Nixon?"

The tech waved, a slight smile on his face. "Hello there. Glad you made it through."

"Do you have any idea —"

"Yes," he interrupted.

Ben blinked rapidly. "That's it? Just, yes?"

Nixon's brow furrowed. "I'm not sure what you want me to say."

"Some sympathy would be nice," Ben said.

"I'd settle for a damn explanation," Morgan countered.

Ben nodded. "Oh yeah, one of those would be good, too. After the sympathy." Another glare shot his way from his partner. Morgan was obviously already feeling better. "Or before the sympathy. I'm flexible."

"Not for another minute or so, I'd imagine," Nixon said. Aggravated groans met his joke. "An unfriendly face from Susan's past decided to pop in unannounced for some revenge. We got caught in the middle."

"The story of our lives with that woman," Morgan said.

"Morgan, this isn't the time."

"No, you're right."

Ben grinned. "I'm what?"

"A pain in the ass." Morgan turned away from him for Nixon. "Is everyone okay?" she asked. "What can we—"

"You can stop with the questions and take these." Nixon held out two pistols. They snatched them from him. The cold metal felt like pinpricks along Ben's hand. "You need to get topside. Now."

CHAPTER TWENTY-NINE

The punch slammed against Metcalf's cheek. Blood spurted from her lips as her teeth sliced into the gum. Metcalf reeled from the blow, but stayed on her feet.

"I'll kill you!" Vivian cried.

Another blow connected, this time to Metcalf's gut. All breath left her. A follow-up strike pounded against her chin, and Metcalf fell.

Her world spun; the sunlight cast halos around the periphery. Metcalf clawed at the earth to crawl away from her attacker. More blood ran from her lips.

"I have to kill you," Vivian said. She trailed Metcalf's slow movements, her hands balled up into fists. "It's the only way I can be free. It's the only way I can live again!"

Vivian kicked out. The blow struck Metcalf in the ribs. She rolled with the hit. Secure in the distance gained, Metcalf struggled to her feet. She cradled her sore ribs, then swiped at the smear of blood on her face. A red stripe trailed from her lips across her cheek.

"You're wrong," Metcalf said. "You're wrong about so much, but you won't listen."

"To what?" Vivian shouted. "More of your lies?"

"You think this is the only way back?" Metcalf asked. "That killing me will bring you closure for what happened? That was ten years ago. What have you done since then, other than hate and pine for revenge?"

Vivian launched at Metcalf. She struck ahead, blow after blow. Metcalf backpedaled out of reach. There was no reason to engage, yet also no reason to endure the pain of another hit.

"I woke up with no memory and no identity," Vivian said. "I was a no one, a shell of a person."

Metcalf caught her fist. "But were you happy?"

Vivian hesitated.

Metcalf threw the fist back at her. "How long were you away? Living this new life?"

"Years."

"In all that time, were you so filled with anger and rage at me for what happened to you?"

"No," Vivian muttered. "I didn't remember. I didn't know any of it."

Metcalf crept closer, her hands open. "Tell me, Vivian. Were you happy?"

"It was a lie," Vivian replied. "It wasn't real."

"It was real to you," Metcalf said. "That life was all you knew. Of course it was real."

Vivian shook her head. "You're twisting things. This is who I am. This is who I have to be because of you."

"Bull," Metcalf spat. "And you know it. Out of a tragedy, you made a life for yourself. You lived in peace for years, away from the missions and the violence and the incredible pile of crap people like us accumulate over the years. You were free of the mistakes, and the judgments for the choices you had to make to survive in this world. Dammit, Ness, you were free."

"It wasn't enough."

Metcalf huffed. "You wasted that peace, that life—your second chance—all for revenge."

Vivian staggered back. Blood dripped from her fingertips. Her hair covered half her face, wild and savage, like the rest of her. She stared at Metcalf, confused and disoriented. A finger ran along her dead eye, dotting it in red from the blood of her enemy.

The vengeful woman screamed. It was too much for her. Everything Metcalf threw at her, the choices both had made over the years, proved too much for Vivian to cope with. She shot at Metcalf with renewed fury. There was no turning back for her—for either of them.

Metcalf dodged blow after blow. She slapped away strikes from the deadly woman, jumped over the swinging kicks, and sidestepped her advances. Every failed connection brought only more anger out of the woman.

"Fight back, damn you!"

She didn't want to. Metcalf, for all her drive and determination, envied Vivian. She had escaped the life, and found a way to forget the mistakes of the past. Metcalf would have given anything to do the same. For all her compartmentalization, for all the secrets she'd tucked in the box over the years, nothing would ever silence the screams in the back of her mind. Nothing would ever wash away the blood on her hands. If only Vivian realized the gift she had been given.

Vivian was right about one thing, though: Metcalf needed to fight back. With every blocked punch or deflected blow, time passed for the others. Ben and Morgan remained trapped. The Bunker continued to be subverted by the external control panel. She didn't even know if Kanigher had made it safely inside, or if Vivian's anger took him from her before she could apologize.

To save her team—her friends—Metcalf needed to end the fight.

"I didn't want this, Vivian," Metcalf said. "I never asked for this."

"Stop talking!" Vivian shouted. All humanity slipped from her until nothing but blood and anger and hate remained. She was more animal-lashing-out than a victim of circumstance. "Fight me!"

"You asked for this," Metcalf said. "Not me."

Vivian snapped. She leaped at Metcalf, hands like claws in front of her. Metcalf sidestepped the strike. She shifted to the woman's right side—directly in Vivian's blind spot.

Confusion and fear ripped through Vivian when she settled on her feet. By the time she turned toward Metcalf, a fist was already flying at her. Metcalf's blow crunched the woman's nose. The force of the strike battered the woman back on her heels.

She didn't let up for a second. Metcalf followed it up with another left cross. Vivian's cheek opened up, and the woman fell to her side. She stopped her descent with her hand. Kneeling on the field, Vivian tried to push her way back to her feet. Metcalf refused to give her the chance. A kick to the jaw dropped Vivian to the earth.

Metcalf blotted out the sun above her, casting Vivian in

shadow. Metcalf leaned over and grabbed the woman's collar. Lifting her up, Metcalf's fist hovered inches in front of the woman's good eye.

"Is this what you wanted?" Metcalf yelled in her face. "I never asked for this life. I never asked to do the things I've had to do. To help people. To make a damn difference. I didn't want this."

"Do it," Vivian spat. "I can't live like this any longer."

Metcalf read the sadness on her face. Killing her would be a mercy. Metcalf was fresh out. She dropped Vivian to the ground and backed away.

"Go home, Vivian," Metcalf said. "Forget me. Forget Hollis and Madrid. Live your life."

For a single moment, Metcalf truly believed it to be over. Vivian sat up. She tucked her knees in close, then swiped at the cuts and scrapes from their fight. She extended a hand, and Metcalf moved to take it.

Vivian turned to her left at the last second. Metcalf's gun lay in the grass at her side. Her hand snatched it up, and she aimed at Metcalf.

"I can't live like this," she said. "Not until you're dead."

Metcalf raised her hands. She stared into the barrel of the weapon, a black hole that seemed to consume her entire being.

The gunshot boomed through the field. The sound crashed against her ears. Metcalf waited for the heat of the bullet to surge through her body. She waited for the pain to settle in, and for shock to take over. More than anything, Metcalf waited to fall.

The gun slipped from Vivian's hand. Blood ran from her lips, and her left eye went as dead to the world as the right. Vivian collapsed on her side.

"What?" Metcalf muttered. A figure stood at the corner of the hillside, gun before him. "Bobby?"

He rushed over to her. Kanigher skirted past the lifeless body of Vivian for Metcalf. He took her hand. "Are you all right?"

Metcalf continued to stare into the dead eyes of Vivian Ness. "I'm okay. It's over now."

CHAPTER THIRTY

The sun set over the hillside. Clouds shifted from puffy white to an array of pinks and purples that ran across the sky in a massive wave. Metcalf stared out the back windows of the farmhouse, weary yet unable to rest. In the distance, she made out the silhouette of Kanigher atop a low rise off the side of the Bunker. He worked tirelessly at his task—digging a grave for the fallen.

They had not spoken since it happened. There had been much to say: gratitude at his rescue, as well as apologies for bringing the menace to their doorstep. Kanigher hadn't bothered to stay to listen to any of it. He had found the dilapidated shed behind the farmhouse. There had still been tools inside from decades past, including a shovel for the task ahead.

Metcalf had tried to talk him down. Vivian's death had been because of her mistake so long ago. While she'd been unable to put the threat down, Vivian had only existed because of Metcalf's previous error. Kanigher hadn't cared either way. Digging the grave had given him the excuse not to join her or the others in the farmhouse, and that had clearly been good enough for him.

Metcalf continued to watch him work, sadness in her eyes. She was unsure how to proceed, how to win him back, or if she even had the right after everything. Turning away from the window, Metcalf made her way deeper into the home. Every creak of the floorboards brought back memories. Every nick in the molding, every notch in the woodwork, all was accompanied by a memory she hadn't thought of in a lifetime.

The others gathered outside the external control room. The wall had been pulled open to expose the hidden space in the home. Nixon tinkered inside with the circuitry. Everyone else, however, remained in the adjacent room—once used for dining. The table and chairs no longer occupied the space, so Ben and Morgan rested along the floor on one side. Adler sat across from them.

All were physically wiped from the events of the day. Though Ben and Morgan missed most of the action, their time in the freezer continued to wreak havoc with their systems. Chills rocked their bodies; the blankets draped over them only did so much, considering the time spent in the cold. Adler's body, on the other hand, appeared unable to cool down. Sweat dotted her skin, and she fanned herself with little-to-no-effect.

They each picked at the sandwiches brought up from the Bunker. Offers had been made to cook, but no one wanted to risk a protracted stay underground after everything that had happened. They needed the change of venue, so Metcalf had brought them cold cuts and bread.

Ben and Morgan scanned the room as they ate. Trepidation filled their eyes, a nervous unknown quality set in from not knowing the farmhouse. The looks turned to anger with Metcalf's arrival. The farmhouse was another secret. External controls had been set by her long ago as a fail-safe, not to be used against them.

She had been wrong about that, just like everything else of late. Locking the doors to the farmhouse had not been to hide the truth from them. It had been meant to keep Metcalf away from the place. This had been her home so long ago, one she'd imagined growing old in with Grissom at one time. If no one else could go home, then she shouldn't either. Metcalf never deserved one anyway.

"I didn't think anything was in here." Morgan swallowed the last of her sandwich, then dabbed at the corner of her lips with a napkin.

Adler nodded. "Same here. I figured it was empty."

"I wanted you to think that." Metcalf leaned along the door frame separating the dining area to the kitchen. A glare shot her way from Morgan. The one from Adler was more of a surprise. Metcalf raised her hand in acknowledgment. "I know. Another mistake on my part."

Ben set down his meal on his napkin. He held tight to the

corners of his blanket and stood. Circling the room, he noted the images on the walls—those Metcalf couldn't bear to throw away. He nearly stumbled at the photo hanging in the corner.

He spun toward her, a finger pointing to the image. "Is that my—"

Metcalf nodded. "Your dad."

Ben shook his head in disbelief. He lifted the photo from the wall. In it, Kenneth Riley put his arm around the shoulders of Metcalf. He wore his bloodstained tie and a proud look on his face. Metcalf was dressed in a graduation cap and gown, her diploma in her hands.

Metcalf remembered the day well. He had helped set her up with school in the aftermath of her abduction. Rather than send her home against her wishes, Kenneth had arranged for a friend to take her in until she was of age. He'd always made a point of visiting, of teaching her something new. He had been the one to bring light back to her world, and she'd wanted nothing more than to be worthy of such treatment.

"You should keep it," Metcalf said.

Ben offered a sad smile. Metcalf understood the complexity of the man's relationship with his father. Family was always difficult, to say the least. She left him with his memories for the moment and turned back to the others.

Morgan worked her way to her feet. She lifted another image from the wall, this one of a young man in overalls and a wide-brimmed hat. "And this?"

"My brother." Metcalf held out her hand. Morgan passed along the photo, and Metcalf ran her finger along the glass. "I left him, ran out on him, a lifetime ago. When I came back... When I finally found the strength to see him again, and ask for forgiveness, it was too late. I... I found him on the floor of the kitchen."

Morgan's hard look softened. "Metcalf, I—"

Metcalf pointed toward the kitchen and the open window to the rear of the property. "That marker out there is his."

Morgan had almost tripped over it during her first visit to the Bunker. It was the night Metcalf had buried Stephanie Atwater. The hill was getting far too crowded.

"He loved this place." Metcalf hung the image back on the wall. "I couldn't let it go."

Nixon stumbled from the control room. He rubbed at his bleary eyes. Everyone turned at his arrival, and the sudden shift startled him. Adler passed along a sandwich, which he gratefully accepted.

"Well," he said, taking a bite. Bread glommed to the roof of his mouth as he spoke. "This Ness person somehow bypassed all the controls. Looks like she took over the system, one section at a time. It must have taken days. If I had known—"

"If any of us had known," Adler interjected.

"You didn't, and that's on me," Metcalf said. "I can only apologize for keeping this from you."

She started for the front door. Ben reached out his hand to her shoulder. "Metcalf—"

"It's okay, Ben." Metcalf turned to face them one more time from the shadows of the front entryway to the farmhouse. Her lip curled in a satisfied grin. No matter their anger at her, they remained her team. "I chose each of you because you're the best for the job. I failed to put my faith in you while demanding you do the same for me. I was wrong. I know you have a decision to make."

The door opened. Darkness threw her into shadow as she left. Her last words echoed through the room. "Please make one, and soon. There's still work to be done."

CHAPTER THIRTY-ONE

Another hour slipped by in quiet contemplation. Nixon finished his meal in quick order to return to work. Adler tried to rest, only to find herself drawn in by the man's fiddling at the control center. Morgan settled across from Ben, the blanket still wrapped tight around her for warmth.

They hadn't spoken since leaving the Bunker. Sure, there had been the unruly burp or two from him thanks to the carbonated beverages that accompanied his meal, but from her there had been nothing of any substance.

They had left things unsaid from their time in the freezer. Ben's commitment to staying with the DSA rested with her involvement, but he didn't know how she'd taken that choice, or what it truly meant for them. The very thought troubled Ben as he searched for meaning in the aftermath of everything that had happened since joining the DSA.

Ben's selfish introspection faded when the door opened, and Kanigher stepped inside. Dirt covered his skin, a bandage wrapped tight to his arm where the bullet had grazed him. His slumped form shuffled through the home, and he set the shovel against the corner before joining the others in the dining area. He made eye contact with only the floor before settling along the wall.

He was a different Kanigher than any Ben had seen during their time together. To Ben, Kanigher always maintained a willfulness that never diminished. He was the stalwart agent who brought his experience to any debate. The man who sat before him now was anything but willful, was anything but strong-minded and ready for action. Kanigher appeared ready to collapse, his spirit shattered from the day.

Adler stopped working with Nixon at Kanigher's arrival. Concern filled her face. She left the control room, made her way over to the leftover bread and cold cuts. Slapping something together, Adler offered the meal to Kanigher. He shook his head slightly, a hand to his gut. Adler persisted, however, and her concern outweighed his petty grievances. Relenting, Kanigher took the sandwich in hand.

"Thanks," he muttered. He picked at the crust for a bit. A small chunk slipped between his lips, and he smiled at Adler. The gesture clearly brought her comfort as relief washed over her features, and she joined him along the wall.

The quiet settled over the room. Kanigher munched while the rest of the team stared blankly at each other. Ben, being unable to let the silence win out no matter the circumstances, leaned forward from the wall.

"All set?" he said, a nod toward the rear window and the task outside.

"It's done," Kanigher replied without looking. He took another bite while he scanned the room. All eyes waited for him. Noting their need, Kanigher lowered the sandwich and swallowed audibly. "So, where are we at?"

"Same place we were this morning," Ben said.

Morgan grumbled and sat up taller. "Apologies don't make up for what she did, Ben. The secrets. The lies."

"No, but forgiveness might be the place to start," Ben responded.

Morgan shook her head. He expected the reaction from her. For as much as she exuded kindness to those in need, Metcalf was a blind spot full of rage for Morgan. She had made up her mind days ago.

"I can't," Morgan said. "I can't forgive her. Not after seeing her with the Witness."

"I'm with Morgan," Kanigher declared.

Ben's jaw dropped. "What? Why, Kanigher?"

"She..." Kanigher paused. His attention returned to the hillside grave, then to the dirt caked to his hands. "Susan's not who I thought she was. Maybe she never was."

"We need her." Nixon returned to the room. He leaned against the alcove wall that hid the control panels inside.

"No, we don't, Nixon," Morgan said.

The tech scoffed. "Look at us. Of course we do. She brought us here. Hell, she just saved our lives."

"From a threat of her own making," Morgan snapped. "She never trusted us, and it's cost us too much. For what's coming? We need to stand as one. That doesn't happen with Metcalf."

Everyone let Morgan's words wash over them. They all tried to reason through them, each with their own argument. Things could never be that simple for Ben. His experiences with Metcalf clouded any anger, or mistrust, for the woman. They gave her a depth Morgan refused to acknowledge, though they all knew the baggage each of them brought to the table thanks to their troubled pasts.

Through the silence, Adler stirred. Her hands clasped before her, and her eyes stayed glued to the floorboards in front of her. "She gave us purpose, Morgan. Thanks to her, you aren't working in some hole-in-the-wall bar. Ben isn't in jail. Kanigher isn't a pawn of the Trust." Her head lifted to meet them. "None of us would likely be standing at all if not for her."

Kanigher reached out to Adler, then stopped. He brought his dirt-covered hand back and wiped it along his pants, to no avail. "I appreciate your opinion, Adler. But you're wrong. Susan—"

"Deserves a second chance!" Nixon exclaimed. "She—"

"Is a liar, Nixon," Kanigher replied. "Open your eyes. I have."

"You think I haven't, Robert?" Nixon said. He moved before the agent, who stood to face the frustrated tech. "Just because she hasn't slept with you is no reason—"

Audible gasps ended the sentence for Nixon. Kanigher, however, grabbed at the man's collar. "What the hell did you say?"

"I merely stated the truth," Nixon said. Cold eyes stared through the weary agent. "Isn't that what we have to do, or face exile?"

Kanigher's grip tightened. "Say it to me again, Nixon, and I swear exile won't be where you're headed."

Ben jumped to his feet. He pulled the two men apart. "Enough."

"You've made this personal, Robert," Nixon said, backing up to the wall.

Kanigher followed suit, an accusing finger pointed at the

man. "It *is* personal. It's our lives! You want to ignore that?"

"I said, enough!"

They swallowed their bitter words. All eyes fell away. Shame replaced anger, then quickly turned to sorrow over their arguments. Stray glances between the team offered silent apologies.

Nixon and Kanigher slid to the floor along opposite sides of the room. Ben continued to stand in the center of the swirling maelstrom created by their debate.

"Ben?" Morgan called, curious.

"No more arguments," Ben said. "We decide now."

"How?" Adler asked.

Ben looked at each of them. The choice had to be made. It was the only way they could move forward. As Metcalf had said, there was still work to do.

"We vote."

CHAPTER THIRTY-TWO

"This way."

A guard prodded Zac and Claire out of the office and into the corridor. He carried a single pistol. No one aided him in his task, the hallway vacant of personnel. That was how little Hollis thought of Zac and his wife. He had spared the bare minimum to keep the pair in line.

Zac wondered if Hollis was correct in that assumption.

"Zac?"

Claire was terrified. She tried to keep her head down, and her steps moving along the corridor. Every few meters, she glimpsed the man's gun. It made her cower, and that weakness crept into her voice.

Zac reached out for her. "Take my hand, Claire."

She cuddled in close to his side. Their fingers interlaced, Zac felt the heat radiating from her. It filled him to his core and lifted his dim spirits. He scanned the hall. They were on the thirty-second floor, along the western side of the building.

When he closed his eyes, Zac saw the entire layout of the structure. He recognized additions made over the years. To their right, two new offices butted up against another for a single department. A new break room took over the entire left side of the hall, where storage had once been kept.

Everything was at his disposal thanks to the programming working its way through his brain, including renovation permits, and the blueprints for each project dating back years. The information covered the whole of the building. Each piece of intel played out in his mind as a possibility, but reality continued to creep back into the periphery.

"They won't keep their word, will they?" Claire's head nuzzled along his shoulder, her words barely a whisper. "You'll do everything they say, and they'll still kill us."

There was no point in the lie. The truth had been evident right from the start. "Yes."

Claire fell away from him. Her hand squeezed harder, though. "I shouldn't have pushed you before," she said. "I should have known there was a reason you couldn't give them what they wanted. Why you—"

"You couldn't have known, Claire." He hugged her tight. He stopped, lifting her eyes to meet his. "I'm sorry I got you involved in this mess."

"Keep moving," the guard snapped.

Zac's gaze narrowed at the weapon. He hated being prodded along like cattle, but not as much as the use of the weapon to make it happen. Claire clearly read his anger and tugged at his sleeve.

"We're moving," she muttered. "Right, Zac?"

"Yeah. We're moving."

They continued for a time through the hall. In the distance, Zac noticed the elevator waiting for them off to the left along the eastern side of the building.

"What do we do?" Claire whispered. "We have to get away from them. If we don't... Oh, God. What about Alex? What if we never see—"

Claire fell to her knees. Her hand slipped away and clutched her chest. Panic took over, and she struggled to breathe.

The guard took aim at Claire. "I said—"

"Don't!" Zac shouted at the guard. "Not another word."

Zac kneeled down in front of his wife. He carried a sad smile, hoping to coax her from the floor. His hand extended. "It's going to be okay, Claire. You're going to see Alex again. I promise."

Claire wiped at her swollen eyes. She smeared her tears along her cheeks. Zac didn't press, he didn't push her, but merely waited. Even through everything, all the sadness and the torture of the day, Claire remained the most beautiful woman he'd ever known. How he had ever let himself forget was a mystery.

The guard, tired of the delay, huffed in displeasure. He pushed past the couple for the elevator.

Zac watched him pass, then stood.

Claire's brow furrowed, confused. "Zac, what are you —"

Zac snatched the guard's shoulder before he could hit the elevator call button. The man spun to meet Zac. "Hey!"

Zac decked him across the face. The man, off balance from his turn, fell back. He tried to lift the gun. Zac launched at the man and his weapon. Both hit the ground hard, rolling from the impact. Grappling for the gun, Zac slammed down his right elbow into the guard's chest. Breath left the guard for a split-second, and his grip slackened on the pistol.

Zac snatched it loose. "Sorry about this."

"Don't," the guard pleaded with wide open hands. "Please!"

Zac spun the pistol around, caught the weapon by the barrel, then drove the handle across the man's face with all his force. The man's eyes closed. Zac clambered back to his feet. "Well, not really sorry, if I'm being honest."

Claire stared in amazement. "Zac?"

He deftly removed the clip from the gun and emptied the lone bullet from the chamber. He tossed the weapon away in one direction, and the ammo in the other, then started for the waiting call button.

"Come on," he said with a nod to his wife. "We have to move."

The doors closed behind them. The moment they began their descent, alarms rang throughout the complex. Zac had hoped for more time — that the guard might remain incapacitated for a few more seconds. Each was precious to his plan.

"Where are we going?" Claire asked.

The numbers fell one by one. When they passed the thirtieth floor, Zac hit the emergency stop button. The car shook from the quick shift.

"Nowhere."

"Zac?"

He shook his head, unable to entertain the question. Zac closed his eyes as he paced the car. His head spun from the options in his memory, one not quite his own anymore. The Wellspring offered solutions on multiple levels, yet each held their own risks. The more time spent within the confines of the programming locked in his brain, the less it hurt him. He hated the lack of pain, almost as much as he did the choices left to him.

Claire's hand halted his pacing. "Tell me what's going on,

Zac."

"Sorry, I was trying to figure things out."

"Then talk to me," she said. "I can help."

"You are," he replied with a smile. She gave him the strength to act. She had brought him so much happiness over the years. It was his turn to return the favor.

Zac took hold of the handrail inside the elevator. Lifting himself up, Zac balanced precariously along the bronze bar. The emergency exit was within reach, and Zac knocked it open. The roof of the car led to the channel that fed from the basement to the peak of the structure.

"What are you doing?" Claire called after him.

Zac peered into the darkness a second longer, the plan still fresh in his mind. He hopped down to her side.

"I made a mess of things, Claire. I'm so sorry about everything. I've loved you since that day on campus. You remember? At the cafe?"

Claire smiled. "You spilled your coffee on me."

They both laughed. "Smoothest move I ever made." Zac took her by the hands. "I'm going to make this right. But I can't if you're with me."

"Too bad." She tried to pull away. He refused to let her go. "I'm not—"

"It won't be safe for you," Zac said. "I... If something happened to you..."

Even between floors, Zac heard the approaching footsteps. Hollis and his men were closing in. It was only a matter of time before the doors opened from their efforts.

"You have to go." Zac reached into his pocket, and removed the note he'd written earlier. He handed it to her. "Here."

"What is this?"

"Instructions." He placed the note in her hand. "I need you to hide and wait until there is an opening to escape. It's Monday, so it will be a while, unfortunately. There will be a momentary gap in their security Wednesday morning at 7:43. You can slip out the rear door."

"Wednesday?" Claire asked. "How can I... Zac, how do you know all this?"

"Please let me finish," he said. "Walk, don't run, from the building. Four blocks west there is a diner. They have a payphone. Call the number on the note. Tell them where I'll be. The location is on the other side. Do this for me."

"I—"

Zac's eyes begged for her help, and they stopped her doubts. "Trust me, Claire." He took her in his arms and kissed her deeply. Zac wished for more time—for another lifetime to make up for this one. "I love you."

Claire fought back a tear. "I love you too."

Zac steadied himself, hands cradled before him. Claire took the hint. She stepped into the cradle and he lifted her up to the emergency exit on the roof of the car. She kicked at the sides of the car for leverage until she was clear on the other side.

"What now?"

Zac pointed into the darkness. "There's a ladder along the right wall. On the next floor, you'll find an access hatch to the ventilation system. You'll be safe there. Remember, 7:43 Wednesday morning. Four blocks west from the building."

Claire nodded, clutching tight to his note. "Come home to me, Zac."

Zac hesitated. He could barely see her through the tears. "I love you so much, Claire."

Hammering on the doors stirred them. Claire rushed to the ladder to begin her ascent. When she had reached the next floor, Zac climbed up the handrail once more. He closed the emergency exit hatch and jumped back down. Hitting the resume button on the car, the elevator shook and continued his descent.

He stopped at the twenty-sixth floor. The second the doors opened, Zac rushed into the hallway. His pounding steps carried him to the southern wall of the building and the windows overlooking the downtown area. Of the bank of three, Zac opened the one on the right. He lifted his leg to the ledge when the sound of clattering steps stopped him.

"That's far enough, Zac," Hollis called. A dozen men stood behind him, all armed to the teeth and looking for any excuse to open fire.

Zac turned to face Hollis. "I won't give you what you want, Hollis."

"I'll find Claire, Zac." Hollis slowly approached. The ring on his finger glinted, the metal spike visible. Zac couldn't help but wipe at the scratch the piece of jewelry had given him. "I'll find her, and then I'll find your boy. All I want is the signal. Give me that, and this ends."

"That's just it, Hollis." Zac pressed tight to the open window. "For all your grandstanding, for all your threats? You need me. But I sure as hell don't need you."

Zac kicked back over the window ledge. His arms criss-crossed his chest, and he fell back into the open air with a smile on his face.

CHAPTER THIRTY-THREE

Hollis rushed to the window. Panic took hold of him, disbelief at the actions of a man he recalled as timid and shy in their first meeting. There was not a suicidal bone in Zac's body, yet Hollis had just witnessed his leap from the twenty-sixth story of the building.

Self-sacrifice was never a quality matched with Zac's demeanor. When Hollis reached the open window, he suddenly realized why.

A grin spread across the man's face. An access tube for a recent renovation project rested directly below the open window. His angle of descent must have taken Zac into the tube, which was used to carry waste down to street level.

Hollis watched the sides of the tube extend and shake from movement. The motion trailed to ground level. Zac slipped from the tube and ran from the construction equipment into the adjacent alleyway, then out of view completely.

A security agent joined Hollis at the window. The rest of the crew kept their distance for fear of reprisal at their apparent failure. The agent stood a head shorter than Hollis, and he ducked out the open window for a closer look at their target's brilliant escape.

"How did he know about the tube?"

Hollis' smile grew at the answer. "He was telling the truth."

"Sir?"

Zac *was* the Wellspring now. It was the only way he might have been able to achieve such an intricate feat. Hollis had kept him isolated, unable to find a clear path out of the building, yet Zac had figured out the layout the second Hollis had dropped his guard. That information was not commonplace. It must have come from the programming filtering through Zac's brain.

Hollis needed that programming. He spun from the window, playing with the ring on his finger. "It was a test," he lied. The damage had been done. Why not take credit for it? Besides, Zac's freedom brought them more than it took away. "A simple test, yet effective enough for my needs."

Hollis removed the ring from his finger. He held it out. A tech slipped through the crowd of soldiers to retrieve the glittering piece of jewelry. It slipped into an open evidence bag. The tech juggled the bag along with his tablet.

"Now to see where the rabbit leads," Hollis said. "Is the tracker working?"

The tech nodded excitedly. "The nanoprobes from the ring are transmitting perfectly."

"Wonderful," Hollis said. "I told you the coffee ploy wouldn't work."

"You were right, sir."

"It always pays to be prepared," Hollis said. The coffee would have been more expedient, but Hollis preferred getting his hands dirty.

"What about the woman?" the security officer asked.

"Right. Claire." Hollis said with a sigh. Searching the building would take time. The woman obviously meant something to Zac, despite the rumors of his philandering. Leverage always helped with people like Zac, and Claire was clearly a pressure point. There was also the more pleasurable option: killing her for being an absolute thorn in his side. Hollis forced himself to admit that the option brought him a certain amount of glee.

So many choices presented themselves, yet none mattered but the end goal. "She's irrelevant," he announced. "There's nothing she can do to save her husband or to stop our plans now."

CHAPTER THIRTY-FOUR

Quiet followed Kanigher through the Bunker. There was no movement in the corridors, no task being accomplished in Operations. All the systems were back up to speed, yet the work remained on hold for the time being.

The team needed the night. After hours of debate, and a vote all knew to be inevitable, the rest of the DSA remained in the farmhouse for the evening. They gathered up enough sleeping gear to make use of the multiple bedrooms throughout the two-story property. They had met any mention of the Bunker with skepticism and concern. It was too soon for them to get back to normal, to push ahead, not with so much having happened over the course of the day.

Kanigher, however, found rest impossible. The vote unnerved him, his own part in the outcome especially. His guilt weighed on him, and rather than sit with it eating away at his gut throughout the night, Kanigher had headed for the Bunker to confess.

Passing through the kitchen, Kanigher almost stopped to prepare a meal. The distraction, though appealing, was merely a stalling tactic, and one he pushed through for the dormitory wing. He didn't know what to say, or how to say it. He simply hoped Metcalf would understand his position and the team's.

Kanigher stopped shy of Metcalf's room. His hand was mere inches from the door, yet unable to commit to that final motion. Too many thoughts swam through his mind. He still felt the weight of the life he had been forced to take to save Metcalf's, and the circumstances of Vivian's anger toward his once valued colleague.

He pulled his hand away from the door and lifted it up for a closer inspection. After washing them multiple times, the dirt remained. The grime was lodged deep under the nails, and caught in minor cuts along his fingers. Kanigher wondered if it would ever wash away, if he would ever feel clean after everything Metcalf had put him through. The truth of the matter still rang in his ears.

She had been part of the Trust. She had taken an active role in their activities, something he had been trying to impede his entire career. Kanigher had believed in the mission — her mission — more than anyone, yet he had never known the truth.

"What a damn fool I've been," he muttered. The words left unsaid remained, and Kanigher no longer wanted them weighing him down. He fought through his trepidation and knocked on the door. "Susan?"

He waited for an answer. None came. Kanigher crossed the hall for the restroom. He knocked twice, then cracked the door without looking within. "Susan? Are you there?"

When no response arrived, Kanigher ducked inside. Emptiness greeted him. Concern grew as he returned to her private quarters. He knocked louder this time, and his voice boomed in the corridor.

"Susan?" He grabbed the knob. The handle gave way and Kanigher pushed it away from the metal frame. The room was empty.

Kanigher stepped inside. The drawers to Metcalf's dresser were open. Her belongings were gone. The duffel bag under her bed had been removed. She had even cleaned out the desk storage.

He tapped his earpiece to activate the comm. "Nixon?"

"Yes, Robert?" Nixon said. The sound of keys tapping in the background filled the line. Sleep was clearly never a priority for the man.

"I had a feeling you'd be up," Kanigher commented.

"There's always something to do," the man replied. "What can I help you with?"

"Has anyone seen Susan?"

"She isn't in the house," Nixon said. Kanigher heard the chair shift across the room. Nixon must have been in the control room already. "I don't see her on any of the monitors either. Why?"

"She's..." Kanigher stopped. His eyes caught something along the back wall. He had questioned her position near the wall earlier that day. She had appeared to be moving her bed, but passed it off as nothing. Now he realized the truth.

Behind the bed, positioned low to the ground, Kanigher found another escape hatch. The seal remained open, and a thin breeze whistled into the room. He couldn't believe it: another secret.

Kanigher stood away from the hatch. Sitting on the center of the mattress was Metcalf's comm link. He lifted it up, then closed his hand around it in frustration.

"She's gone," he said.

"Gone?" Nixon asked. "What do you mean? Did you tell her about the vote?"

Kanigher tapped his earpiece and ended the call. He sat down on the edge of the bed, his eyes on the thin stream of darkness peeking through the open hatch. Whispering a prayer for her, Kanigher hoped she might find what she was looking for out in the world.

He chuckled when he recalled the vote and the reason for his arrival. "I guess she made her own decision," he said in the empty room. "Typical."

CHAPTER THIRTY-FIVE

The duffel bag hugged her back. Metcalf pushed through the cold, harsh current of wind. Darkness surrounded her, the shadows of night her only company along the road.

She had made the same trek decades earlier. Both times offered her no clue as to the destination. The future remained unknown, the path ahead clouded by the mistakes of the past. With all the years between, the entire time spent making up for that first mistake, Metcalf was still running away.

She didn't need to hear the team's decision. The debate, no matter where it landed in the end, never should have occurred in the first place—not if she'd been doing her job correctly. Metcalf took to the road to avoid another argument, but more to maintain control over her own fate. It was the same problem that started the situation, the same difficulty that caused her to walk the path alone in the dark.

The team would move on from her. Metcalf had chosen them wisely, brought them into the fold because of the strength of their character, and their need for redemption. They would see the DSA through the dark times, fighting for the answers the way she had taught them.

Metcalf needed to find her own now. It was time for her to strike a fresh path. The mission, however, remained the same; everything she did, and would ever do, was for the betterment of the DSA. The work was too important.

It had been from the beginning.

They buried the inquiry. Too many questions had been raised

about Anson Greene, too many problems left unresolved by the accusations brought to bear by his murderer. If the public ever found out about Greene's true work, of the dubious deed that brought about his end, confidence in the government would shatter.

Never-ending probes would exacerbate the situation; the sound bites played on every major news network ad nauseam. Instead of opening the Pandora's Box of political nightmares, the Board of Inquiry tucked everything related to Greene's demise in a neat little box, and buried it in the wasteland of history.

Maybe the board's actions were justified. Metcalf, however, remained uncertain—even in the face of a full vindication for her actions. She worried the act of hiding the truth merely covered the board's own complicity in Greene's work.

All Metcalf knew was that two men helped clear her name: Jacob Grissom and Robert Kanigher. Despite the tension of their first meeting, both men stood by her side during the inquiry to offer their perspective of the crime. They informed the board of Greene's duplicitous actions against the stars and stripes, his death necessary to save lives.

She was grateful for their help. She had spent her entire life working alone. It was a pleasant change of pace to have someone next to her.

Dismissed from the inquiry, Metcalf headed out without a clue as to her future. With Greene dispatched, Metcalf wasn't sure how to proceed. Questions continued to rattle around her brain. So many, in fact, Metcalf paused outside the inquiry theater. She made her way over to the large picture window overlooking the Capitol.

She leaned against the glass, her head resting along her arm. The Trust was gone—as dead as its figurehead. The threat she had been fighting against was no more. In return for her efforts, her record had been cleared of any wrongdoing, her past washed from the system. Nothing stood in her way, and the options ahead were limitless, yet questions continued to plague her.

"Why, Greene?" she whispered under her breath. "Who was that old woman in Madrid? What were you really after?"

"Too many questions," a voice said from behind her.

Metcalf pushed off the window and turned to face the newcomer to the conversation. She had thought herself alone, the hallway clear when she'd entered mere moments earlier. Standing in the center of the corridor was a lone figure. He wore a black suit and fedora. A small smirk was the only marker of his intentions as a thick pair of round spectacles hid his eyes.

"You should follow them to their answer," the man said. He joined her at the window.

"Who are you?"

He smiled wider at the question, like he had heard it a million times before. "A simple witness."

"That doesn't explain anything."

He nodded, yet never peered in her direction. He simply stared out into the gloom over Washington. "There is a way, you know. A way to learn the truth. A way to make a difference for the future."

"How's that?" Metcalf said with a laugh. "I don't think they'll be accepting an application from me in this lifetime."

"They have short memories, and the work you do will change their minds quickly."

The work? The idea intrigued her. "What's the job?"

His opaque spectacles swallowed her whole. "Tell me, Susan Metcalf. Have you ever heard of the DSA?"

Metcalf followed those questions and formed a team around her. It started with Grissom, then grew to include so many others along the way.

Kanigher refused to commit at first. His loyalties were to the NSA, but he quickly came to see the truth beneath the surface. He always believed in her.

It took years, but Metcalf built the department from the ground up. She outfitted her people with the latest in technology and weaponry, all in the hopes of staying ahead of the enemy. Her entire purpose had been in service of answering the growing list of questions that trailed her every move.

Her answers remained elusive.

Metcalf tucked her head down and continued along the dark road out of Odenton. The only way back to her team was to find out the truth. It was the only way to keep her people safe, and to end the fight she'd started so long ago.

ACKNOWLEDGEMENTS

A special thank you to my incredible patrons:

Matt Patrick
Sally Hall
Sara Frandina
Paul Sardella

Your support means the world to me and I could not do this without you in my corner.

This book would not have been possible were it not for my lovely wife, Melinda, who always keeps the story straight even when I don't.

I also cannot forget the great feedback from my wonderful friend, Vicki Wilkinson, who was immediately upset with me about this book and made the reveals so much better because of her reading experience.

ABOUT THE AUTHOR

Lou Paduano is the author of the Greystone series of urban fantasy adventures, which follow Detective Greg Loren and Soriya Greystone as they hunt myths, monsters, and legends in the city of Portents.

He is also the author of the conspiracy thriller series, The DSA, a serialized tale about a clandestine government agency trying to discover the true power behind humanity's future.

Lou lives with his wife and three daughters in Grand Island, NY. You can learn more about his books, including upcoming releases and free content by visiting his website at loupaduano.com.

THE GREYSTONE SAGA

AVAILABLE NOW

Follow the adventures of Soriya Greystone and
Detective Greg Loren as they hunt dangerous
myths and legends in the city of Portents.

BOOK ONE - SIGNS OF PORTENTS
BOOK TWO - TALES FROM PORTENTS
BOOK THREE - THE MEDUSA COIN
BOOK FOUR - PATHWAYS IN THE DARK
BOOK FIVE - A CIRCLE OF SHADOWS

GREYSTONE-IN-TRAINING

AVAILABLE NOW

For years, Soriya trained to become the Greystone.
Follow the trials that made her the protector
Portents needed to fend off the darkest of threats.

BOOK ONE - HAMMER AND ANVIL
BOOK TWO - THE GIFTS OF KALI
BOOK THREE - THE FINAL GAUNTLET

THE DSA CONTINUES IN…

The Wellspring.

This ancient program has guided the world down a singular path toward a future which remains a mystery. At the heart of this program lies a signal, transmitting instructions to chart the course ahead.

Zac Modine has finally found the signal. Unfortunately, the Trust has followed his every move, and under the leadership of the manipulative David Hollis, they will stop at nothing to secure the future for their own ends.

The DSA is all that stands in the Trust's way. But will their timely intervention help save the world from the threat of the signal and the dangerous guardian at the gate, or will they merely open the door to a power beyond all comprehension?